HOME AT LAST

JOHN H. RHODES

PUBLISHED 2021
JOHN H. RHODES

ISBN 978-1-7330126-1-4

Editor

Ashley Middleton Davis

Developmental Editor, Cover Design, and Formatting

Michelle Morrow, Chellreads.com

Dedicated to those who returned from the Vietnam War with PTSD, and those who lost their lives and didn't return.

I wish to thank the members of the South Beach Writers Group, especially Ms. Linda Schaeffer for the encouragement I received while writing this story.

I also wish to thank Ashley Middleton Davis for the many hours of editing she did during 2020 while living during the threat of a one hour time limit to evacuate due to forest fires, and also living under the coronavirus shutdown with her two small children while confined in their small home.

I also wish a special thank you to Michelle Morrow for helping me make this book the success it is. She was so helpful editing the manuscript along with many suggestions she gave.

Last but not least, I couldn't have written the story if it wasn't for the many Vietnam veteran friends and acquaintances who have shared so many of their experiences and other information I was able to use as background information concerning the treatment of so many veterans upon their return to the U.S. including the symptoms and issues PTSD created for them.

HOME AT LAST

1

CARL

1979

Carl Weston pulled his old pickup truck off the main highway onto the gravel drive that accessed the upper reaches of the Weston Ranch. Knowing the gate would be locked, he came prepared. He had a bolt cutter and a newly purchased paddle lock. He got out of the truck, cut the chain securing the gate and added his own lock. After he drove his pickup through the gate, he re-locked the gate. With both locks attached, he would have access and by leaving the other lock attached, other family members would retain access also. With the gate locked, he drove on into the ranch property till he was overlooking the large valley that made up most of the ranch's upper grazing lands along with the mountainous foothills surrounding it.

Arriving at the cabin, he discovered it hadn't been lived in for a long time. Just as he hoped. The cabin had been built so two ranch hands could live there during the summer while the cattle herds were being grazed in these high meadows. The ranch had CB radios in their four-wheel drive vehicles so nobody was sent to stay in the cabin anymore. Once inside, Carl spent the rest of the day cleaning the house and by evening, found coffee, a coffeepot, and was able to make a pot of coffee. He would have loved to have a beer, but he didn't have enough money for it.

Carl poured himself a cup of coffee and walked out onto the porch, sat down, and watched the sunset. He was actually able to relax knowing he'd finally arrived at his destination, he was home at last. His mind wandered; How many years had slipped by since he'd last been to this cabin. These higher fields weren't used in the winter because the cattle were moved to the lower grazing fields in the fall, and not moved back till summer. The cabin was in a valley accessed by four miles of gravel road. Carl wanted nothing more than to be able to crawl into a hole and be left alone. The last thing he wanted was to have to deal with people who wouldn't understand his condition.

Between his gravelly voice, and his no nonsense attitude, the less he had to deal with other people the better. The cabin would fit his need perfectly. Well secluded and few visitors. If there were any visitors, they would be from the main ranch, and would be family. Carl purposely left the existing lock on the gate so any member of the family could get through. He wasn't looking forward to that day, but he didn't want to lock them out either. It was their land, so didn't want them calling the law on him. As it was, once his cousin Fred discovered he was living here, all hell would break loose.

While enjoying the coffee and the sunset, Carl's mind went back over the previous years.

At age five he lost his mother and father the night their home burned. Damn, he was five, but the burning home was forever seared on his mind, never to be forgotten and relived in many childhood nightmares. He often wondered: by the time he was ten, would he have had a brother or sister? Would he have been a good big brother? Would he have had a happier childhood?

An aunt and uncle took custody of him and their son, his cousin Fred, couldn't get along with him. Maybe it was a personality clash. Both middle school and high school had been hard and he was always in some kind of trouble. He never did anything wrong, but nothing seemed to go right. During that last year of school, he got expelled and sent to a military school. At eighteen and graduated, he wanted to put home and his past behind him, so he enlisted into the Navy. He couldn't shake the feeling the rest of the family was overjoyed knowing he wouldn't be their problem child any longer.

Once in the Navy, he was shipped out to Vietnam while serving on a destroyer. He was later transferred to a small PBR (Patrol Boat River) patrolling the Mekong River in the delta areas where the larger Swift Boats couldn't go. Running the river in a speedboat would have been fun but all too often they encountered Charlie--North Vietnamese guerrillas-- trying to smuggle equipment on the river or on the shore.

Stopping all suspicious boats--mostly canoes or sampans--and destroying any war materials found wasn't bad duty, but they often encountered ambushes hidden on shore. These inadvertently included a firefight lasting as long as it took to speed by and call in helicopter gunship support. He always put the engines at full throttle while they returned fire. They never went back to see what got left behind, that was left up to the helicopter crew. Carl felt he had the best seat on the boat, back with the engines rather than at the helm or at one of the two machine guns. Their last patrol didn't go as it should have.

As we rounded a bend in the river, Charlie was waiting, hitting us with everything, killing both gunners and the helmsman. The boat hit the shore and to this day Carl didn't know how he got ejected from the boat into the river. As he was regaining his senses, Charlie was pulling him from the river. He was now a prisoner of war. For Carl it was the beginning of hell where the devil was going to get his due and Carl was going to pay in spades.

Carl recalled marching for miles, and eventually his captors put him in a Viet Cong prison camp with other POWs. The food was lousier than lousy and the treatment worse. After a year, seven of them started planning an escape. Other prisoners tried to dissuade them because if they did escape; they'd be hunted like dogs and shot. Yes, Carl could remember scoping out the camp every chance he got when let outside to march, work, or stand in the rain being miserable. Oh man, Carl could remember the day of their escape; they needed a diversion. Making absolutely no noise to alert the guard, he creeped up behind him and, with sweat running down his face from the humid Vietnam air; grabbed the guard's neck. With a quick twist, he snapped it like a twig. Carl could feel his own blood running through his veins as he felt the guard's life drain from him. As he lowered the dead guard to the ground, he grabbed one of the guard's grenades and flipped it into the closest building and ran for the hole under the fence. Fear of missing his chance of freedom made his all-out run a marathon. He had to make it to the location where the other six prisoners would be one by one slithering under the fence. Carl could still hear Roy's dying scream as he was shot while crawling under the fence. The six of them ran for the jungle, and most of them headed east. It would be a long way to friendly lines, so Kyle and Carl circled the camp and headed west for Cambodia. The idea was the Viet Cong would search for the men running east the shortest way back to their bases.

Hiding and hiking the jungle and the mountainous terrain was a grueling trip. Carl could still remember the two of them stumbling upon a Viet Cong outpost, and finding a man present. Carl crept up on him and like the guard at the prison, snapped his neck. Carl was wearing the man's clothes, and weapons on his way out of the camp and thought; how ironic the Viet Cong destroyed my clothes, beat me till I soiled myself, put me in the hole, and killed my shipmates, and this guy gave me his clothes. When his comrades find him, they will have to put him in his grave.

Before Kyle and Carl reached the border, the Viet Cong was hot on their trail, so they split up, Kyle headed south and Carl continued west. Carl often wondered if Kyle made it back or not. Finding the way through the jungle was hell. Having no idea of how far he'd traveled, he found a house in the jungle. What a jack pot, he cautiously entered the house, found nobody was home so helped himself to the food he found and took some of the clothes so he could get rid of the Viet Cong uniform and firearm. Cambodia wouldn't welcome a North Vietnamese soldier, so he would trust his fate to being a civilian. His dog tags had been taken from him in the prison camp, so while in foreign countries, he was a person without identity. The trick was to evade any police or other authority figures.

As Carl continued to watch the sunset, he remembered walking half-starved into the outskirts of a little fishing village on the coast. After helping a fisherman fix the engine on his boat and ingratiating himself, the fisherman invited Carl to go fishing with him, figuring Carl could keep his engine running. He fished with this man for a year until the topic of his going farther south was broached. Carl was also trying his best to learn the language too. While working with several different fishermen, he was able to work his way south to South Vietnam, all the time helping them keep their boat engines running and helping them fish.

It was in a small village in South Vietnam where fate or maybe it was his lucky star intervened and put him on a Chinese woman's small trading junk. She traded between towns and cities along the coasts of Cambodia, Thailand, and Malaysia.

It took two years to work his way south to Singapore.

There he worked in a Chinese operated warehouse and dock away from prying eyes. Carl worked like a dog for the man, but it was an odd arrangement. The man, a Chinese, had Carl work for him in a warehouse off the docks where fishing boats docked to unload. The authorities never came around the hot stinking fish packing docks. It was while working in the warehouse his leg got hurt. It wasn't broken, but the Malaysian doctor who treated him could have done a better job treating him. Carl ended up with a slight limp, but he never let it slow him down. After working in the warehouse for a year, he met with the skipper of a Panamanian freighter that was sailing for Manila, Philippines, and on to San Francisco.

Carl reflected on his time aboard the destroyer which was where he learned how to repair all types of small engines. If it hadn't been his Navy training, he wouldn't have been able to work his way from Cambodia to Singapore, much less home. While working aboard the freighter, Carl took care of maintenance of the lifeboat engines and the many pumps on board which had been allowed to fall into disrepair. He also took on duty in the engine room. The ship's first port of call was Manila; he didn't get off the ship, not wanting to take any chance of being detained for any reason. When the ship docked in San Francisco, Carl hid so no questions would be asked by the customs agents who came onboard. He joined a group of the ship's crewmen as they went ashore after dark but never returned to the ship. This was arranged with the skipper, who gave Carl an advance on his pay. It wasn't the total amount he had coming because it was forfeit due to his being homeless. Damn, the skipper made out like a bandit because the rest of his wages would be sent to the ship so naturally the skipper would get to keep it.

After some time spent working farms with other transient field workers, Carl was able to buy an old pickup truck. He stayed long enough in the Frisco area to get an apartment, got a job cooking in a greasy spoon restaurant, and finally a fake ID card. Using the fake ID, he got a driver's license and started north, finally reaching the family ranch in Montana.

As the sun went down, Carl was home, seventeen years after leaving and thirty-three years old. He was pleased with his timing; fall was a few days away, and the cattle were no longer grazing in these upper meadows because they had now been moved to the lower ranch fields. He wouldn't be expecting family visitors until next spring or summer when the herds would be moved to these upper meadows again. Well, the north cabin was home enough since he wouldn't be welcome at the main house. *Hell,* he thought, *I won't be welcome here either once Fred knows I'm living here. But damn, I joined the Navy in 1964 at eighteen, escaped the prison camp in 1970 at twenty-four, and here it is, 1979 and I'm thirty-three.*

Home at last and welcome as the plague.

2

CONNIE

While driving home from the county fair, Connie wondered why her friend Donna asked about Carl. Everybody knew he was reported as MIA so what was there to ask about? It had been a long day for her two boys, Bill and Mike both now asleep in the car with her.

Connie recalled the last time Mike asked about Carl, it was during dinner several years back. That conversation hadn't gone well, Connie recalled her husband, Fred's answer. "Last we heard he was in Vietnam and the Navy notified Mother, your Grandma Carol, he was either a POW or MIA."

"What's that?" asked Mike.

"Prisoner of war or missing in action," Fred replied.

"You mean he might be dead?"

After a long silence, Fred commented, "The war ended in 1975 and until then he was listed as a POW but once the prison camp was liberated and Carl wasn't there, they listed him as MIA."

The rest of the meal was eaten in silence.

Connie went on to recall asking Fred while they were getting ready for bed, "What happened and why was Carl sent to *that* school?"

Fred explained, "Carl was always in trouble, fighting, doing everything he shouldn't, he caused the family nothing but trouble."

Connie asked, "Oh my, did he ever go to jail?"

"No," replied Fred, "he never broke the law, but he did everything else to cause trouble. One time he was going to work on the tractor and it ended up costing Dad a pretty penny to fix. He wrecked the hay truck and swore it was an accident. He was in fights at school on a regular basis. One time he shot the neighbor's dog and swore it was trying to kill the chickens. I had to go to school with him to keep him out of fights and trouble. I still remember Dad blistering his butt for going swimming in the river. We were never allowed to go there. A lot of kids went there to drink and party. It was popular with kids but several kids lost their lives in it over the years. He finally got expelled from school for fighting in the classroom. He broke the other kid's arm and nose. The day Dad sent him to the military boarding school was the best day of our lives."

As Connie pulled into the driveway and parked by the large ranch house, she woke the boys and got them headed into the house and to bed. She took a couple of minutes to smile and appreciate how happy she was. She and Fred had married in 1964, had three children: JoAnn, William, and Michael. JoAnn, the oldest, was now twenty-four and from a previous marriage of Connie's. William, who preferred being called Bill, was ten, and Michael, nine, preferred being called Mike.

It was a happy year when she and Fred moved out of the family home and started their own family. Fred was nine when, his mother and father took in his cousin Carl who had lost his mother and father when their family home burned. Fred and Carl's fathers were brothers, making the two boys cousins. Since Carl was a cousin but treated like a son by Fred's parents, Fred had to take on the position of older brother but for some reason the two boys never got along well.

Connie went on to remember two years after she and Fred got married, Fred's father passed away. Two years later, Fred's mother, Carol, had health problems and moved into the assisted living home in town. Fred had the old ranch house razed and a new large modern home built. Connie loved her new home and it made living on the ranch so much more comfortable for the family.

As Connie changed her clothes for bed, Fred walked into the room so she reminded him, "We should go visit your mother sometime. I think we should try to visit her more often." "Yeah, well the ranch won't run itself." He grumbled.

"Donna surprised me when she asked about Carl. I think they knew each other in school." was Connie's attempt to get more information from Fred.

Fred barked, "What brought him up? You have JoAnn's wedding to help plan, two boys who need help with their schoolwork, and a ranch to help run. What are you worrying about Carl for?"

Connie thought, It's odd how nobody seemed to worry about Carl, being a POW or MIA wasn't a good thing, no matter who it was. She asked, "How did your mom take Carl's being reported MIA?"

"She doesn't talk about it." Fred grumbled as he climbed into bed.

The topic was never broached again. They were busy with the ranch, so they seldom ever visited Fred's mother. That was another issue; they should get into town to see the boy's grandmother but the three kids, housekeeping, and helping with the ranch ate up her time.

After showering and combing her hair, Connie wanted to get to bed and get some sleep; the next day was going to be another long one. She smiled to herself knowing if the boys didn't raise and show animals at the fair, she wouldn't get any time away from the ranch. She treasured each minute she shared with her friend Donna whom she only got to see while at the fair.

3

DONNA

Being the beginning of fall, the county fair was preparing for opening so Donna was helping set up various displays. She loved to volunteer for the fair and it became an annual affair for her. She loved helping arrange the produce and vegetable displays and any other items needing some extra attention. There was no end to the extra little details needing to get done before the fair opened. This was her second day helping and as lunchtime approached, her friend Connie stopped by. The two women first met while working at the fair and since then, made it an annual time to renew their friendship.

As Connie approached, Donna greeted her with an enthusiastic, "Hello." Connie embraced Donna with a hug and replied, "Let's go get some coffee and a bite to eat, I'm famished." At this same moment, her two boys, Bill and Mike arrived and Sharon, Donna's daughter, excitedly started hopping about. Sharon loved getting to go with the two older boys and have a chance to get away from her mother for an hour. "Can Sharon come with us?" the boy's asked?

"Yes, she can go with you but she has to stay with you and be back at 1:00 PM." The two women watched the boys walk out of the building with Sharon skipping along beside them.

Connie looked at Donna and commented, "They will take care of her, and they sure get along together."

"Yes, Sharon looks forward to spending time with them." Connie asked, "How have you been, is life treating you well?"

Donna replied, "Yes and work has been nice. We have several new teachers at the school and they are really nice." "You're Sharon is sure growing, how old is she now?" asked Connie.

"Eight and keeping me so busy I don't have time to sneeze. Sometimes I wish you and I could see each other more often. I know Sharon would like that too."

Connie replied, "That would be great but we're so busy on the ranch, we never get into town."

"I know, with my working at the school every day, the

only time I can get any housework done is on the weekends. The boys are a year older than Sharon, right?

"Mike is nine and Bill is ten."

"What are the boys showing this year?" Donna asked.

"Bill is showing a cow. Mike is showing a pig and a goat." replied Connie. "Raising the animals, caring for them, feeding them, transporting them, and keeping them ready for the show is real work but the boys love it. It also keeps them busy and out of mischief."

"Sharon looks forward to her time with them also." replied Donna.

Connie commented, "Fred can be difficult at times but do you ever miss being married?"

"A help mate would be great but not a guy who isn't nice. I'd love to have a forever guy in my life who loved me but I don't see that taking place any time soon." replied Donna as her memory went back to her married years. *Bert, her husband had been sweet until after they had Sharon, then he turned into a different person and treated her like dirt. She couldn't do anything right and Sharon was an obstacle, it was as if he hated the baby and took it out on Donna. She also remembered how happy she was at graduation from the community college and her wedding a month later. She still couldn't understand what happened, was she too young and naive? Sharon was born the following year and Bert turned into a different person. Rather than the nice, sweet guy he had been, he made life miserable. She wanted a happy home for Sharon, so got a divorce. One year after the divorce, Bert was killed in an auto accident on the interstate. Though she divorced him, she still wouldn't wish his type of death on her worst enemy*. Donna shook her head to clear it of these unhappy thoughts and turned her attention back to Connie.

As they finished their coffee, Connie commented, "We'd better get back; we don't want the kids to get there before us." Connie's remark made Donna smile and agreed.

THEY MET for lunch the following day and after an enjoyable time of visiting, they headed back to their respective showing locations.—Donna and Sharon went to the produce barn and Connie, Bill and Mike to the animal barns.

While walking back Donna remembered asking Connie about her husband's Brother Carl. What was it, a couple years back and Connie told her he was listed as MIA. They weren't real brothers but Donna didn't know what the real relationship was. He lived with them for as long as she could remember. He was a year older than her and in a different class but she remembered him because back in grade school, she had secretly liked him.

He never spoke much, but the one thing she did remember was while in high school, he saved her brother's life. A bunch of kids had gone to the river to swim. Her brother was grounded for a month for doing it, and he never told his mother or father what really took place. Donna remembered that evening while in her room, her brother came in and confided in her, he told her Carl was the one who jumped into the river and pulled him to shore. It was quite a surprise because her brother and Carl were several years apart in age and didn't know each other. She remembered her brother telling her, "The point is, Carl isn't as bad as what most kids say he is."

She never told her brother she had a crush on Carl in grade school. She was a year younger than Carl so not in the same grade. In grade school she always wore her hair in pigtails. She liked to swing beside him whenever he was on the swings. The trouble was. He was always proving he could swing higher than any of the other kids, and of course, Donna was scared to death to ever try to swing as high as Carl.

Donna's mind was pulled back to the present as Sharon asked, "What are we having for dinner?"

"I'm not sure, probably leftovers from last night."

"Mom, I'm not hungry, do I have to eat?"

"So what did you eat at the fair?" Donna asked,

knowing the kids ate at one or more of the food vendors kiosk's at the fair.

"I had a hot dog and strawberry shortcake with Mike and Bill." replied Sharon.

"Well I'll have to speak to their mother about that." Donna replied sternly while inwardly smiling to herself. *What child could pass up eating goodies with their little friends?*

THE THIRD DAY of the fair proved a long one for Connie and the boys so she talked Donna into joining them at a local restaurant for dinner. While eating dinner, Connie commented, "I sure miss having friends to chat with. We're so busy on the ranch and out so far, I don't get many chances to get away. Helping the boys with their projects is the only way I get away."

Donna could understand though working at the school she had plenty of interaction with others. Once more her mind wandered back to those school days. *While in high school, Donna wasn't one of the popular girls, but she didn't lack for friends. She got along with most of the high schoolers, but she didn't try to compete with the popular girls or cheerleaders. The boys on the football team were like knights of old, a class unto themselves who dated the popular girls. If you weren't popular or a cheerleader, you might as well have been invisible. Though she didn't have the same childhood feelings for Carl while in high school, she still respected him. She didn't know what took place, but the team members, never talked to him the way they talked to other students. She recalled being told he beat up several of the team members, but she didn't know that for sure. It bothered her when a friend told her he was expelled from school. The rumor was he broke a classmate's arm and nose.*

On the drive home after dinner Donna couldn't recall Carl's name ever being mentioned unless she asked. *Were they hiding their loss by not talking about it or did they see his absence as a blessing? What put a thought like that in my mind?* Donna was brought back to the present by Sharon's question, "Do I have to take a bath tonight, it is late, you know."

"You smell like the animals so you need to wash. Let's take a quick shower together and off to bed we'll go." replied her mother.

4

THE CABIN

Carl found the cabin well stocked with non-perishable food but it would run out so he'd need to do something soon. He contacted the Veteran Affairs and applied for his military discharge, but that would take time. He also got a part time job at an auto shop in town, so he could afford groceries. While working at the auto shop, he seldom went into the front office because he didn't want to have to talk to any of the customers. Once in a while, a friend of one of the crew might come back into the shop to chat, but those he could usually ignore if he was busy working on a vehicle.

Since he wasn't paying rent, water, garbage, or anything else at the cabin, he didn't need much. When he wasn't working at the auto shop, he performed maintenance on the ranch buildings, and if time allotted, went for hikes to re-discover the lay of the land.

Carl wasn't interested in looks or anything that didn't have a purpose or make his life easier. His clothes were plain and he preferred work boots to the fancier cowboy boots many people wore. Carl wore what most people referred to as combat boots. In his mind, why bother with high heel, pointy-toed shoes when one wasn't spending any time on horseback?

He couldn't understand the arrogance so many men had when it came to the shape and brand of their large, broad-brimmed hats either. The boonie hat he wore was perfect for jungles or any hot weather. It had a broad brim for protecting his face and eyes, and vents allowed a cooling effect for his head while still retaining some heat. Those big cowboy hats did neither of those.

Carl didn't care for people who felt they had to add fancy gates with fancy signs announcing a family's name to their ranch's entrances. It was all such a charade; something to make others think you were better than the next person. After having the crap beaten out of him--literally--then living with so many fishermen while making his way back home, it didn't make sense to him why the people needed so much unnecessary materialistic stuff. How many times had he eaten food he couldn't identify during those years? Yet it was good. Granted it wasn't a steak done to perfection, but it was good, nonetheless.

In his mind, if you have food and a roof over your head, all is good. The cabin provided all of these and the gate three miles away provided the privacy. That's all Carl wanted.

His biggest demon was his own mind. The flashbacks and nightmares were enough to drive him crazy. He hated those nights he would awaken from a dream reliving the time he was in the prison camp. On those occasions, no matter what time of night, he had to get out of bed, make coffee, and sit out on the porch, to get his mind back to the present. It was hell waking with his heart beating like a drum, breathing as if he'd run a marathon trying to avoid being caught by informers or Viet Cong soldiers while escaping the prison camp.

One day at the auto shop, a customer was telling the other mechanic of his need for money and was willing to sell a rifle he had. Carl looked at it and made him an offer. It was a 1917 Enfield 30-06 and the fellow was selling it cheap, so Carl purchased it and later in the fall used it to kill a deer and an antelope.

WINTER WAS APPROACHING, and Connie sent JoAnn to town for groceries and some parts her dad needed. On her return trip, she thought, *I wonder if the north cabin is ready for winter. Maybe I'll swing by and take a look, though it's out of my way.*

She liked to drive and didn't feel like hurrying home right away.

After turning off the highway and while stopped at the gate, she was surprised to see a second lock on the gate's chain. Obviously, somebody was accessing their property. She unlocked the lock her key fit, drove through, relocked the gate, and drove on in. She crested the hill and could overlook the valley and saw a pickup truck parked beside the cabin.

It was starting to snow, but the first snow of the season was always a light one, so she didn't need to worry about it. Besides, she wanted to discover who was at the cabin and why they were there. She stopped her car and called her mom on the CB radio.

JoAnn asked her mother, "Do we have any employees at the cabin?"

"No, why?" her mother replied.

JoAnn explained, "There's a pickup parked beside the cabin. I'm wondering who might be there." She added, "I'm going to see who's there."

Connie said, “Oh my, you be careful and call me right back.”

“Okay, Mom.”

JoAnn parked in front of the cabin and gave two knocks on the door and walked in.

Carl saw her car at the top of the hill so knew somebody was coming. While wondering what family member it would be, he conveniently made sure he was seated at the kitchen table with a cup of coffee and a book he was reading. Well, it would look like he was reading.

A young lady in her early twenties walked in after two knocks and brusquely asked, “Who are you?”

Carl asked her, “Who are you?”

The young lady replied, “I asked first, and this is our cabin.”

Carl had given a lot of thought to what he would do when discovered. He knew his face was scarred from the patrol boat crash, his voice was now a low gravelly growl due to damage done while at the prison camp, and his right leg gave him a bit of a limp after being hurt while working in Singapore. Carl said, “I’m Kyle. By any chance would your name be JoAnn?”

JoAnn was totally shocked and asked, “How do you know my name?”

Carl explained, “While I was in Vietnam, I had a good

friend. His name was Carl and he told me if I ever needed a place to stay or live, I would be welcome to stay here."

JoAnn didn't know what to say or believe. This was too much for her. She didn't know enough about her father's cousin Carl to ask many questions, so she decided to discover what she could. The strange man eventually offered her some coffee and told her of his serving with Carl on the river patrol boat and their capture.

The story had its twists and half-truths, but Carl wasn't going to have JoAnn run home and tell her dad his wayward cousin showed up. To JoAnn, he was a man with a scarred face, walked with a limp, and spoke with a low, rasping voice. They talked for several hours and Carl didn't press her and let her ask the questions.

He also explained, his "good friend Carl" told him his brother had a daughter. "Let's see, if I recall, that would be you. It's been so many years; it's hard to remember everything he told me." Carl wanted to ask if she had any brothers or sisters but didn't want to feed her with any information relating to him by letting her know what he didn't know.

All JoAnn could think was, *How else would Kyle know of the family*?

She asked, "How did you know how to find this part of the ranch?"

He also explained, "Carl gave me a great description of how to get to the cabin."

"Why didn't you come to the main ranch house and ask if you could stay here?"

"Carl told me that wouldn't be necessary, come right in. If any questions were asked, tell them I'm a friend of Carl's." Carl knew this would drive his cousin Fred crazy but also figured it would be something his cousin would expect him to do.

By this time it was snowing extremely hard and JoAnn decided it was time to leave. She went to get in her car and discovered the snow was too deep for her car to ever make it to the top of the hill. She got frightened and tried to radio home but couldn't get through on the CB. It wasn't unusual because of some hills between the upper ranch and the lower ranch. The lack of radio reception between the upper and lower ranch areas was probably one more reason they didn't have employees living in the cabin during the summer when the cattle were in the upper fields.

She asked the stranger--Kyle, she remembered his name--if he could help get her car to the top of the hill for her or maybe pull it. Carl explained, "My truck is two wheel drive and being so light in the back end, couldn't make the hill either.

JoAnn fretted and complained, "The first snow of the year is never this bad. What am I going to do?"

Carl said, "There's two bunks in the back room and plenty of bedding in the linen closet; you're welcome to stay a day or two."

JoAnn was beside herself, but Carl made sure she had everything she needed and fixed them both a dinner. At bedtime, told her he was going to be seated in the easy chair in the front room so she could get ready for bed, and the top bunk was available. His was the bottom bunk.

JoAnn informed him he could go to bed and she was going to sit up all night. She was not going to be sleeping in the same room as he was.

"Suit yourself," said Carl, and he went into the bathroom and got ready for bed and turned in.

Three hours later, JoAnn could hear Kyle snoring in the other room and decided she would climb into the top bunk. She wouldn't go to sleep but she could at least relax and rest for a few hours.

The next morning Carl had pancakes ready, woke JoAnn, and informed her coffee and breakfast were ready.

JoAnn felt awkward knowing she had fallen asleep.

Kyle also commented, "I see you couldn't resist sleeping while listening to my nightly lullaby."

The snow had stopped, but it was still too deep. She was still stranded. By now she knew she was safe and hoped her mom and dad wouldn't be too worried and send a search party. That would be embarrassing.

While sitting and waiting for better driving conditions, Kyle asked JoAnn how Carl's mother was, adding, "Carl talked about her good cooking, so I was kind-of wondering."

JoAnn said she wasn't his real mother but an aunt, and she was living in the local assisted living home.

After spending a second night at the cabin, the weather warmed and rained. Carl drove her car to the top of the hill since she was leery of trying it herself but still wanted to get home. Carl agreed that neither one of them wanted a search party sent looking for her.

It was a mile to the top of the hill where Carl let JoAnn drive the remaining three miles to the highway. The two miles to the gate and the last mile to the highway were relatively flat so they both knew she wouldn't have any trouble. It was three miles from the cabin to the gate and one more mile to the highway.

She had her own key so could unlock and relock the gate.

As soon as JoAnn drove through the gate and locked it, she called her mother on the CB and told her she was safe and leaving the gate. She also added, there's a Navy friend of Carl's living in the cabin. "I'll tell you about it as soon as I get home."

JoAnn's mother walked across the porch to meet her as she drove in. Connie gave her daughter a big hug. "I was so worried, we almost sent a rescue party out!"

JoAnn explained, "Mom, the man at the cabin knew Uncle Carl in Vietnam." JoAnn always called Carl uncle since he was close to her father's age, and nothing else sounded right. She said he treated her well so she couldn't complain. He seemed nice. She went on, "He fixed meals for the two of us and told me a lot about his friend, you know, Uncle Carl."

Later when Fred came in, he inquired if the cabin was damaged in any way. JoAnn explained, "No, in fact, for a bachelor, he kept the dishes clean. Yes, the place was lived in but not trashed. I didn't see anything wrong but was probably too upset to notice."

After JoAnn went to her room, Fred turned to Connie and said, "This is exactly the kind of crap Carl would pull. With winter coming on, I don't know when we can get in there to run the guy off. That's our summer cabin for people to stay in when we put the cattle in those upper fields."

Connie couldn't help thinking, *When was the last time we sent an employee up there to stay?* She didn't vocalize her thought to Fred.

5

THE LAND

1980

As early spring brought better weather, Carl drove to town and stopped at the assisted living home. There he inquired which room Mrs. Weston lived in. They wouldn't give him her room number till he explained he was a friend of her son Carl and he served with Carl during the war. He thought it would be nice to stop by and talk to the lady about her son. It was the best story Carl could think of, and in some respect, it was true. They finally gave in and allowed him to walk to her room.

Upon knocking on the door, he heard her answer with a "Come in," so he did. She was sitting in a chair with a book. Carl introduced himself as Kyle Thompson and gave her the same story he gave JoAnn. Mrs. Weston listened to his tale and asked for more specifics about Carl. He answered all of her questions except telling her anything that would blow his cover.

He asked her how often her family came to see her. She said not often. She informed him it was a mutual agreement, she didn't want to live with them and they didn't want her living with them either. After an hour went by, Carl said goodbye and would return again soon.

Every Thursday evening, Carl stopped in to see his aunt. She liked his visits because it broke the monotony; besides, she liked the company. After several weeks, she asked if he would arrive earlier and have dinner with her. While at dinner--what there was of it in this establishment--his aunt asked where he was staying. He told her his friend "Carl" had given him the directions to the upper cabin with a *carte blanche* invitation to stay as long as he wished because the family wouldn't mind.

Carol couldn't help herself and said with a laugh and big grin, "Oh, I'm sure they won't mind."

After four months of his religiously visiting, Carol, his aunt, was fairly sure Kyle was Carl. A mother knows these things. Though not being his biological mother, raising him from age five was much the same thing. She knew he was Carl. Granted, his face was scarred, his voice was a raspy croak, and he walked with a slight limp, but why the ruse?

During his next visit, Carol asked Kyle, "Since you say you're a friend of Carl's, why do you come to see me?"

Carl didn't have a good answer for this, so he didn't try.

Carol continued, "I don't know why you're calling yourself Kyle, but I know better. I know you and Fred never got along, but the family's going to find out sooner or later, you know this."

Carl didn't leave that evening till quite late. He described his prison escape and explained his need to work with fishermen and other boatmen of whichever nation they belonged to as long as they would get him closer to home. He was a POW, but when the prison was liberated at the end of the war and he wasn't there, they listed him as MIA. It took years to get home, and being penniless, he wanted a place to crawl into, any place where people would leave him alone. "Nobody knew where I was living till JoAnn discovered me at the cabin," he said.

Before he left, he asked Carol not to spill the beans. Carol's response was, "This is the most exciting thing that's happened since I moved in here; why would I do that?"

As Carl drove home, he wondered if Carol would rat

on him and tell the family, or maybe, she'd forget this evening's conversation. He didn't give the last much credence because he knew she was sharper than that. Carl also wondered what part of his cover or story gave him away, much like leaving the second port on Chi Lou Mei's boat.

After leaving port, the next morning he woke and couldn't find his shoes. Granted, his combat boots were next to worn out but they still fit. All he could find was a pair of Chinese shoes where he had left his boots. He looked all over and finally asked, "Momma San, where's my boots?" He didn't know Chi Lou Mei's name at the time and though he couldn't speak Chinese, she knew what he was asking. She pointed to the Chinese shoes several times till he got the idea to put them on and when he did, Chi Lou Mei indicated her approval. It took him a few hours to realize she had thrown his boots overboard because his boots could and would give him away at some point. While in the first port, he wondered if she would turn him in to the authority's or keep him. She didn't need him but he needed her. His job was to make sure she felt she needed him. It took time but he managed to make her understand he was an asset by keeping her boat's engine running.

It was during this same month Fred paid a visit to the cabin and told Carl he couldn't stay. He would have to leave because two of his employees would need the cabin. Kyle replied," "Carl told me ranch hands no longer used it since there were better roads now.

His answer infuriated Fred. "I don't care when it's used, you're a freeloader trying to take advantage of my property."

Carl pointed out, "I'm not taking advantage, and I've made improvements and repairs."

May was bringing nicer weather, and Connie ran into Donna in town.

They had coffee, and Connie told Donna about the man who was staying at the cabin and asked if she would mind going with her for the ride to the cabin.

Connie was curious and would like to meet this friend of Carl's but she didn't want to go alone, though she didn't want to go with Fred.

Donna said she understood and would go with her.

The two women arrived at the cabin and Carl was aware somebody had arrived. He was in the barn fixing stall gates. Granted, no animals were using the barn, but if they ever did, the stall gates would need repaired.

The two women knocked on the cabin door, but there wasn't any answer. They walked around the cabin and heard Carl in the barn. After entering the barn and approaching the man, Connie introduced the two of them. "Hello, I'm Connie Weston, and this is my friend Donna."

"Hi, I'm Kyle," he replied as he reached out and shook each woman's hand. "Let's go to the house; I'm sure you want to talk."

He put his tools down and led the way to the cabin, opening the door to let them in. Carl asked if they would like anything to drink, but both declined.

Donna looked nice with a plain face devoid of any makeup. That appealed to Carl. Her shoulder-length hair looked nice too, quite satiny. The modest dress she wore had a small flower print and shape that in his mind, accentuated her femininity. *Oh well,* Carl thought, *I'll probably never see her again.*

Carl noticed Connie was several years older than Donna and knew she was Fred's wife. She also looked like she had aged a bit, which wasn't a surprise since he knew through discussions with Carol, Connie was raising three kids, helping run the ranch, and dealing with Fred. Connie appeared as if she had taken time to look nice but a busy day had taken its toll.

After declining anything to drink, Connie thanked

Kyle for being so kind to JoAnn when she got stranded. Connie was quite direct and asked what he was doing in the barn. Carl explained how the place had been left to deteriorate, so felt the least he could do was get the discrepancies squared away. Connie asked how long he was planning on staying at the cabin.

Carl said he didn't know. *Forever, but I can't tell you.*

She tried to inform him of her husband's desire for him to be gone as soon as possible. She also asked as many questions as she could think of about Carl. He answered some and others he said he didn't know or couldn't remember.

She also asked, "When was the last time you saw Carl?"

Carl told her, "It was after we escaped from the prison camp and Charlie was on our trail so we had to split up."

"Who was Charlie?" Connie asked.

Carl explained, "At that time, it was Viet Cong soldiers, the communists. Hell, for lack of a better name, Charlie's what we called the North Vietnamese soldiers and any of their sympathizers."

While answering Connie's questions, Carl wondered if his friend, the real Kyle, ever made it back alive like he did. He also thought, *I may never find out, so I'll use his name.*

Connie wanted to ask him about his voice and leg but

chose not to because if his voice was a birth defect, it wouldn't be appropriate.

While driving back, Connie asked Donna, "Do you believe him or not?"

Donna was surprised at the question and asked why Connie wanted to know.

Connie said she didn't know. "Call it a woman's intuition, but something isn't right. I just feel it."

Donna asked Connie, "What part of his story don't you believe?"

Connie replied, "I'm not sure, but I'm not convinced he's telling us everything. What's your opinion or first impression?"

Donna said, "I never expected him to invite us into the house, much less offer us anything. I was expecting him to be confrontational, so his dropping everything he was doing to talk to us was a surprise. I'm not sure if he knew we were coming or not, but he knew you were the property owner. Like I said, I was expecting a confrontation and he was anything but. He wasn't rude during our visit. You said he was good to JoAnn while she was stranded with him for a couple days. This tells me he's not a jerk and not trying to hurt anyone."

Donna had her own thoughts but kept them to herself. She had liked Carl when she'd known him before the war, and MIA was like being lost, and no closure. She'd not given it much thought but being somebody she liked; it made her sad thinking about it. She also noticed the family didn't lose any sleep over it either. She never talked to Fred, but from what she got from Connie, there wasn't any love lost when it came to Carl. Donna couldn't understand families like that because she was close to her brother. She also had Carl to thank she still had her brother since he'd saved him from drowning all those years ago.

DURING DINNER FRED commented with a concerned voice, "Next week we have to move the cattle to the upper range and I hope Kyle doesn't try to stop us."

"Why would he do that?" replied Connie.

"I don't know but I'll bet he'll try something, God only knows. We have Carl to thank for this crap. He was always a problem and now I still have to deal with him. One would think he's come back to haunt me."

"Fred, I think Kyle knows we put the cattle up there in the summer so I don't think he'll mind. Just because he's living in the cabin doesn't mean he will try to stop us using the range land." commented Connie.

"What do you know, we don't have any idea what that man will do. If he harms any of the cattle, he'll be in town talking to the sheriff and judge about his incarceration. I'll make damn sure of that." Fred interjected.

Carl stood out on the porch and watched the cattle streaming into the field on the opposite side of the drive from the cabin. More out of curiosity than anything, one of the ranch hands came over to see what Carl's reaction would be. "What do you think?" he asked trying to open a conversation and discover if there would be a confrontation. "Those are fine looking animals." was Carl's gravelly reply.

With the coming of spring, Carl tilled a plot of ground behind the house and put in a garden. He planted vegetables, squash, carrots, onions, corn, and potatoes. His one big concern was whoever saw the garden would know he was planning on staying for an extended amount of time. That or put two and two together and figure he didn't plan on ever leaving.

As far as he was concerned, he didn't have a choice. He didn't have enough money to attend school, and being so long struggling to get home, he was years behind all of his peers in the workforce. That and the fact he didn't know his situation with the Navy; he was still listed as MIA, so he wasn't officially discharged yet and that could take years to solve.

From his experience, everything the government did always took more time than it should--well, unless it was their collecting taxes from you. He was hoping he could get a Montana driver's license without a big hassle. The fewer questions asked the better. He didn't want to try and cope in the rat race of middle-class working society for many reasons.

First and foremost, his voice, looks, and bum leg wouldn't be an asset. The ugly thought of having to put up with people or crowds, both of which he avoided so ranching would suit him just fine. His dream was to live in the valley away from the rat race, the daily competition between people trying to get more than they need, or better than the next person. He'd stay in his valley and cope with his nightmares and flashbacks. The worst ones were reliving the beatings and treatment in the prison camp.

During one of Carl's visits to his aunt, he saw an invitation on her table. "What's this?" he asked.

"Read it." He did, it was an invitation to JoAnn's wedding with time and place.

Carl commented, "Oh, you'll be going, won't you?"

Carol said, "Probably, providing they come and get me. Why don't you come and get me. You'll be my plus one. I do believe I'd like that."

Carl replied, "That should create quite a stir."

Carol added, "I like the idea. Do you have any

appropriate cloths to wear?" "No, not really, but..." was his answer.

THE FOLLOWING WEEKS VISIT, Carol gave him one hundred dollars and told him to get something to wear to the wedding.

Carl was shocked, and questioned his aunt, she looked him in the eye and said, "Carl, I don't know why you're posing as Kyle, but I know better. Why are you still using the ruse?"

The only thing Carl was able to say was, "I feel it's better this way. Fred doesn't have to know who I am. You know as well as I do there'd be hell to pay if he knew I was living at the cabin."

"I understand," said Carol and left it at that and added, "Get yourself a pair of slacks and a nice shirt."

6

THE WEDDING

Carl pulled into the parking lot to pick up Carol hoping she wouldn't have too hard of a time getting into his pickup truck. It sure wasn't new, but it was all he had. Carol was ready and when he got to her room, she commented on the nice shirt and bolo tie he was wearing. As they walked into the church, Bill and Mike clambered to see her. She gave each one a hug and kiss while Carl was having a discussion with one of the ushers. They were to seat the guests, but rather then one of them taking Carol to her seat, Carol put her arm on Carl's arm and with her cane in the other hand, walked slowly to the second row of pews and took a seat. A few minutes later the family was being escorted to their seats.

Connie stopped and gave her mother-in-law a hug and said she was happy Carol was able to make it. She also gave Carl an odd look and asked, "Oh my, did you come together?"

Carol replied, "Yes." and left it at that.

Connie was surprised and while thanking him for bringing the kids' grandmother, wondered--*How did those two meet?*

After Fred walked JoAnn down the aisle and took his seat, he turned to Carl and said, "Why are you here? You weren't invited."

Carl responded, "Somebody had to bring JoAnn's grandma."

During the ceremony, JoAnn happily glanced at her family and was shocked to see Kyle sitting with her grandma. Being in the middle of her wedding, it was lost in the excitement.

During the reception after the ceremony, JoAnn hugged her grandmother and said she was so happy she was able to attend. She looked at Kyle and gave him a quizzical look.

"Congratulations," Carl said with a big grin, "Do I get to kiss the bride?"

Before JoAnn could answer, Kyle was giving her a big bear hug and kissed her cheek.

At least I get to give my niece a kiss on her wedding day, Carl thought.

After all the people congratulated the parents, Connie

was able to stop by where Kyle and Carol were seated and said, "It was so nice of you to make it, Carol. I see the two of you have met; how did that take place?"

"It's a small town, Connie," was Carol's response.

That night, Connie pondered the situation. She was sure something wasn't adding up with Kyle and now, she was sure. She couldn't help wondering how those two had met. Something wasn't right. She didn't know if she should be disturbed, angry, or frightened, but a frightening thought entered her mind. *Is Kyle actually Carl? It can't be since Carl was reported as MIA, but who is Kyle? He can't be Carl because Carl doesn't have a mess of scars, a limp, or a gravely, croaking voice. What stories did Kyle tell Carol, and does she believe them? Is she convinced he is genuine?* This was a disturbing thought. Connie still couldn't accept they met and befriended each other. *Hopefully,* Connie thought, *Surely Kyle doesn't think he can live on their land for ten years and then try to claim it as his own.* They would have to run him off before that took place. Needless to say, she didn't sleep well that night. Worry and her spinning mind kept her awake.

During the following month, Connie devised a plan. First off, she was certain--well almost certain-- Kyle couldn't possibly be Carl because Carl was reported MIA. She would need to talk to Kyle again to see if she could determine if he was telling the truth or not and determine if he was a detriment to the ranch. He was actually making improvements since he was doing maintenance where needed. *Why is he doing it?* was also a question she couldn't answer. *Most intruders or squatters ruined a place so why is Kyle actually fixing things? Was he planning on staying for a long time, maybe forever?*

The second week after the wedding, while Carl visited his aunt, she told him she had some papers in the top drawer of the dresser. As he removed them from the drawer for her, she told him to read them. Carl was shocked to see it was the land title or deed to the upper half of the ranch.

He looked at his aunt and said, "You didn't have to do this."

"Fred will never allow you to stay on the property so you have to outright own it. This assures you half the ranch. The lower half will be Fred's, though I haven't given him clear title to it yet. This way, you each legally own half the ranch.' The two of you will have to learn to work together but that's up to the two of you, I've done my part."

7

THE MEETING

Once more Connie made arrangements to be in town, meet with Donna, and drive to the cabin. On the way, she told Donna about Kyle attending JoAnn's wedding with Carol. "I don't know how he discovered who or where she was, but it couldn't have been a coincidence. I want you to be with me as my friend and as a witness. Oh my, I'm genuinely concerned about this guy. I don't believe he is who he says he is." Connie also told Donna of her worries; all those fears she couldn't dispel from her mind about Kyle.

After they arrived at the ranch, Carl invited Donna and Connie to sit on the porch with him since the weather was nice. Connie came right to the point and informed Kyle he wouldn't be allowed to stay on the ranch. The cabin was for employees.

Kyle mentioned his friend Carl told him employees weren't using the cabin anymore, so he could stay as long as he wished. He wasn't trying to be a freeloader and was trying to fix anything he could, providing it was within his budget.

Connie asked what he had been doing between the war and his arrived at the ranch.

Kyle answered he worked at odd jobs in California, but times got more and more difficult. As money got tighter, he could see he wasn't getting the jobs he needed, and he'd soon be homeless. So it was time to take his old friend Carl up on his offer. Yes, he thought there might be problems since he waited so long to do it, but, he tried to make it on his own and it didn't work out.

One thing Carl didn't do was tell her how he managed to return to the States after escaping the prison camp. By leaving those details out, it made it sound like he had been in California for all those years rather than working his way from Cambodia to California the hard way. The less she knew the better.

Connie still wasn't convinced, much less put at ease. She still didn't trust Kyle; what was he not telling her?

Donna could understand her concern but didn't know how to help. One suggestion she offered was to pay him as an employee, and as long as he performed maintenance on the buildings and equipment, he could stay. That would give them time to investigate him further. Donna couldn't explain why, but for some reason she wanted to get to know Kyle better. She also realized Kyle would never be a friend of Connie's, so she shouldn't get in the middle of a family problem. But what was it? For some reason, she felt a connection with the guy. She hoped she'd have a chance to see him again.

Connie approached Fred with Donna's idea but presented it as a way they could later fire Kyle and they would be legally able to evict him from the property. It would also give them time to see what more they could discover about him.

Two weeks later Connie and Donna drove to the cabin to see Kyle. Once more, he greeted them and offered coffee. Connie explained, "Since you are doing maintenance on the buildings and fences for us, and not trashing the place, I've convinced my husband to pay you a small salary."

Carl profusely thanked Connie for going out of her way to help him. The salary would sure be helpful. Knowing there was only so much work he could do on the buildings. He broached the topic of the tractor and old hay truck. Neither ran any more, thought he could probably make them run but he couldn't afford their parts. If he was assured of being reimbursed the cost of the parts, he could get them back in running order.

Connie had to think about this but decided it wasn't a bad offer and accepted. During part of the conversation, Donna walked out onto the front porch needing to walk away and think about the situation her friend Connie was in. She crossed the porch and wandered around to the back of the house. Wow, she saw the lush green cultivated rows; it was obvious Kyle had put in a large vegetable garden. She intuitively knew how much work that entailed and not something anybody would do if they thought they would be leaving soon. She returned to where Connie and Kyle were and asked, "Connie, have you seen the garden out back?" Connie walked to the back so she could see it and was surprised too. Connie couldn't get beyond the feeling that everything was out of control and she didn't know what to do or think. She could only hope she was doing the right thing.

While driving back to town, Connie discussed everything with Donna and gave voice to all of her worries. She also hoped Fred wouldn't make her the object of his anger when he discovered she was negotiating with this homeless squatter. There was that other fear and she almost hated herself for voicing it to Donna but asked, "What if he actually is Carl? I don't believe it's possible because Carl's MIA, but we don't have any idea of what actually took place in Vietnam? Oh my, is it possible for an MIA person to come back home unannounced?"

It was too much for Donna to take in. Her tummy did a flip-flop, a strange feeling engulfed her, suddenly goosebumps covered her arms and shoulders.

Connie added, "I'm sure it's not possible, but my intuition is telling me Kyle isn't telling us everything. He was over there and has an answer for everything. I'm worried sick and he frightens me. Not because he's mean, but because I don't trust or believe him. What's he not telling us? I have this terrible foreboding and I can't get this frightened feeling out of my head."

Donna was out of suggestions and didn't know what to say to her friend. She couldn't help believing he was Kyle because the Navy would have notified the family if Carl was not MIA. She also had to admit to herself, as Connie had put it, there was something about him that didn't add up. Something else also bothered her, why did she get such a strange feeling when she was near him? This last she didn't like admitting to herself because he wasn't flirting with her or trying to ingratiate himself to her, so what was the attraction? Why was she always happy to see him? Donna couldn't answer any of these questions but the strange feelings bothered her.

THE NEXT TIME Connie visited the cabin was with the two boys, Bill and Mike. As they were getting out of their car, Carl asked, "Did Donna come with you?"

Connie ignored his question because the boys were noisy and excited since they hadn't been to this part of the ranch for several years. They enjoyed talking to Kyle as he told them he was going to fix the tractor and hay truck. He was going to take them apart and see if he could fix them. Mike asked Kyle, "Mom said you were in the war with Uncle Carl. What was your job?"

Carl explained he was the engineman on board a PBR, a thirty-one-foot river patrol boat. His job was to keep the pair of roaring 180 HP Detroit diesel engines running and make the boat speed up and down the rivers while patrolling for enemy troops and smugglers. The faster the boat ran, the better everyone liked it. They loved the story and, in their minds, saw a speed boat racing on a river with machine guns blazing.

Carl couldn't put a finger on why he asked Connie where Donna was. Actually, he just blurted without thinking, and he couldn't explain it to himself. She seemed nice, but she was Connie's friend. He would never get to know her. He wondered if she attended the same school as he did and if yes, what class would she have been in. *Well, I'm not going to lose sleep over it.*

Connie had stopped by to discuss tractor parts, truck

parts, and their reimbursement, and the boys wanted to meet him and see the outlying area. Once they got home, she phoned Donna and told her Kyle had asked why she didn't come too. Donna didn't know why, but there were those butterflies in her tummy again, so she asked Connie if she could accompany her the next time, she went to see him. Connie wondered why Kyle asked about Donna. Did he think her a witness because Donna always accompanied her when she would otherwise be alone? That had to be it because they didn't know each other. She thought, *Oh my, does he like Donna? No, that would be absurd.*

8

THE GARDEN

Donna accompanied Connie on her next visit but couldn't decide why she wanted to go. On the drive to the cabin, Connie mentioned that her mother-in-law had passed away. She didn't know when they would schedule a service, but it wasn't going to be right away since she was going to be cremated. After some small talk, the topic finally changed to Kyle's vegetable garden, and both Connie and Donna wanted to see it again.

Once more, after arriving at the cabin, the three of them found themselves sitting on the front porch. After chatting for a few minutes, Donna asked when he was planning on putting up the produce.

Carl said, "Probably this coming weekend, why?"

Donna wasn't sure why, but she asked, "Would you like

me to help you with the produce? It will take a lot of work to bring it in, wash it, and prepare it for canning. Do you have a pressure cooker?"

Carl said, "I can do it." for some unknown reason, he added, "I suppose I could use the help. I have a pressure cooker but if you have one also, we could double up and get done faster. When would you be able to get here?"

"I'm the school secretary, so it can't be a weekday. How's this Saturday?"

Carl replied, "That will be fine, I'll be up at zero eight hundred to unlock the gate so you can get in."

Connie couldn't believe what she was hearing but didn't interrupt. Donna was right; it would take a long time to prepare all the produce. It was sure nice of Donna to make the offer. Donna was as surprised as Connie when she blurted her offer to help with the garden's harvest.

Donna couldn't leave her daughter home alone, so she told Sharon, "We're going to spend the day on a farm. I won't have time to play because I'll be helping Kyle can his vegetables." She made sure Sharon had several books to read, a coloring book, crayons, and a puzzle. She wasn't sure how Kyle would take to having an eight-year-old present, but she wanted to see him. She wanted to get to know him better and find out what he knew about Carl. Besides, he might as well know she had Sharon. She got a strange feeling as she asked herself if she was attracted to him. Well, was she attracted, or was it something else? She didn't know why she enjoyed his company. She wasn't sure why she offered to help him with the vegetables but there was that strange feeling again.

Carl had coffee on and was already starting to harvest the vegetables and get them ready for washing. Once Donna got Sharon situated in the cabin's front room, she took over washing the vegetables. Carl picked and brought them in, and Donna washed them and either set them aside for storage or in a different location for canning.

On one of the trips in Carl stopped and asked Sharon, "What's your name?"

Sharon looked at him and informed him her name was Sharon and she was working on her brand new puzzle. "Mommy got it for me yesterday."

Carl looked at the picture and said, "It will be a great picture when you finish it." He turned and headed back to the garden.

After a while, Sharon trotted out to see what was taking place in the garden. She noticed there were lots of worms left exposed from Carl's digging up the potatoes. She became concerned for the worms when she saw several Robbins grabbing them and flying off. She started picking up the worms so they wouldn't get hurt or taken by the birds. He finished with the potatoes and Sharon returned to the cabin and started coloring.

It was quite late when they finished canning and Sharon had fallen asleep. Donna wanted to ask Kyle a thousand questions but didn't know how to begin. She was too self-conscious to ask the questions.

Carl finally asked her, "How good of a friend are you of Connie's?"

Donna said, "We met at the county fair years ago but don't get to see each other at any other time. "Your arrival has upset Connie a great deal, and from what I understand, her husband too. She needed a friend, a neutral person to talk to. You're arrival has upset her so much, she's overwhelmed. Why?"

Carl didn't answer but couldn't help wondering if Donna was being used as a spy so to speak. He commented, "Your Sharon looks like you."

Donna felt she had to take the leap and asked. "Can I see you again sometime?"

Carl said, "I suppose, but you can't get in here because the gate is always locked. There's no phone and the only communication is by CB and it only works from the high points such as at the top of the hill."

Donna thought a minute and asked, "If it's nice next Saturday, let's have a picnic. I can bring some hot dogs and stuff."

Carl thought a minute and couldn't think of any reason to say no, but he wasn't much for company. He sure wasn't comfortable in the presences of women and was self-conscious of his looks. He knew he didn't win any beauty prizes and his voice didn't endear him to conversation, which he kept to a minimum and to the point. He also didn't have much time for the social conversations women liked to hear. He didn't know what to expect, much less why Donna wanted to have a picnic with him. There wasn't anything for a little girl either. Well, they could use the fire pit behind the house and he had plenty of wood so they could have a bonfire. *Kids love bonfires, so he was sure Sharon would enjoy it,* he thought. "Well, if you like, I'll get the fire pit ready so we can have a fire outside," Carl said.

"Sharon will love that. We can roast hot dogs on it too," Donna replied.

9

THE PICNIC

Saturday morning Carl was awake by zero seven hundred and after breakfast drove to the gate to unlock it. He didn't know when Donna was going to arrive, though he didn't expect her till after noon.

Donna and Sharon arrived at 12:30 PM. Carl helped her unload the food and carried it into the house. He apologized profusely for not having anything to contribute. He hadn't gone to town except to work.

Sharon helped with what she could and asked if she could go outside. While outside, she explored the old garden, the fire pit, the tool shed, and the barn, the tractor, and the old hay truck. She liked sitting in the cab of the old hay truck. While Donna got everything ready, Carl lit the fire, and put a pot of camp coffee on to boil. Carl found some chairs so the two of them could sit and chat while they enjoyed the fire and the coffee. Sharon occupied herself but not without asking Carl tons of questions about the farm. He informed her it was a ranch, not a farm, and explained the difference. It didn't escape his notice she didn't differentiate the difference and continued to call it a farm.

After hot dogs, baked beans, potato salad, chips, and watermelon, he was stuffed and didn't want to move. It was a great feeling sitting there with coffee and watching Sharon play in the dirt of the tilled garden. She was one busy girl, but eventually she went into the house and fell asleep in the easy chair.

After sitting by the fire for a while, Donna finally raised the nerve and asked him where he grew up.

Carl was quiet for some minutes and didn't want to lie to her, so he didn't reply. Knowing she expected some answer, he replied, "Home wasn't the loving family one would normally believe, so when I got the chance, I left and joined the Navy." It was a half-truth, as close as he could keep it to the truth without letting her know who he was. After that, he reverted back to his past story, being in 'Nam and serving on the PBR patrol boats. Between being blown out of the boat and the treatment in the prison camp; he was marked for life, his face, his voice, and his leg; what the hell. "One thing though, I can still work on stuff, but it takes longer now," Carl said.

"Do you ever go into town besides for work?" asked Donna.

"I've been working part time at the auto shop, but otherwise, only when I have to. You know; groceries and parts, I don't need anything else," commented Carl.

He couldn't bring himself to explain he wanted to be by himself. He didn't want to go into town knowing what people would say, much less how they would react to him. Some of those people were classmates who treated him like dung in school, and he didn't so much as want to say "Hello" to them. As it was, he was Kyle and not Carl, and that's how he wanted it. They weren't worth his time, and besides, he was aware of the ideas people had concerning returning vets.

He'd run into those people in California after he returned. He could tell who was a veteran and who wasn't. He seldom talked to other veterans anymore after listening to their experiences. Returning so many years after the war, the animosity wasn't as pronounced; though it still existed. Being called a baby killer and being treated like scum weren't part of his desires. He didn't have to put up with it and didn't know how he would react if it did take place. He could understand the anti-war sentiment, but not the way so many people treated the veterans. The veterans did their job, the job they were drafted to do, and so many didn't get to return.

Donna went into the house to check on Sharon, and Carl followed her. He asked what grade Sharon was in. Donna answered, "Third grade."

Carl commented, "She seems happy and plays well by herself."

"Yes, but she keeps me busy," Donna said. "It's getting late and I have to get Sharon home to bed."

Carl noticed it was long past a third grader's bedtime so helped Donna pack the leftovers to the car. After everything was in the car, he carried sleepyhead Sharon out and put her in the car. Carl thanked Donna and told her he enjoyed the picnic and the day. He wanted to include "her company," but thought better of it and thought, *I wouldn't mind giving her a hug but I don't want to be too forward.* As Donna got into the car, he told her he would follow her out and lock the gate.

While driving home, Donna wondered if Kyle would ever contact her. She had helped him can the vegetables and invited herself for the picnic she provided. *Would he reciprocate in some way or was she wasting her time.* She couldn't put a finger on why but she liked him and loved spending time with him but she needed to know how he felt. *Granted, having Sharon complicated things, but she's my life, Sharon is everything to me.*

10

CAROL

Carl got word his Aunt Carol had passed away; he found the mortuary in the phone book, called and ask for information on Mrs. Weston's memorial service and burial. After some stalling, they finally told him the date and location since the information was already in the newspaper.

The day of the service, Carl didn't sit in the back pew but did sit behind all of the other attendees. A few minutes after he got seated, Donna came in and joined him. Carl couldn't help thinking: *Oh damn woman; you sure know how to make my day difficult. This isn't going to be easy. The next several hours are going to be an emotional rollercoaster for me. I loved Aunt Carol and she's the only person who ever saw my side. I was gone for seventeen years, and now she's gone. This isn't going to be easy, so I wish you weren't sitting beside me.*

After the service, Carl, with Donna riding with him, joined the motorcade to the cemetery for the internment. After the short service, the urn was left on a green platform so the cemetery crew could actually bury the urn after the family and friends left. Carl stood at the graveside after the others started walking away.

Donna got halfway back to the truck and realized Kyle wasn't with her. She stopped, turned and looked back; he was still standing at the grave. She continued on to the truck to sit and wait for him. Fred, Connie, and the boys had gotten into their car when Fred noticed Kyle still at the grave. Connie wondered if Fred was going to confront Kyle, which she didn't want him to do, so she placed her hand on his leg.

Carl was lost in his own thoughts. Aunt Carol was the mother he'd known since he was five years old. She took care of him, so he found her death a real loss. He knelt and moved the urn and its platform to one side. He put the urn in the grave, picked a few flower petals from one of the bouquets, and dropped them on top of the urn. He scooped up some earth and let it run through his fingers down onto the urn. Finally, standing scooped up another hand full of dirt and let it rain onto the urn. Carl thought,

Ashes to ashes, dust to dust, and to dust we shall return. The Lord knew she had finished all he had for her and had called her home. Damn, he would miss her. As he slowly walked back to his truck, he thought, *Thank you, O Lord, for allowing me to return before you called her home.*

While Connie and Fred watched Kyle at the graveside, Connie reasoned, Kyle isn't just a friend. No friend of a friend would attend his friend's mother or aunt's memorial service. Instantly the thought struck her, *Oh God, he can't be Carl*! A cold sweat swept over Connie and she honestly felt fear. *What was going to happen? Oh my, he couldn't be Carl, he's MIA.* Once more, she knew in her heart, he had to be Carl. She wondered, was Fred thinking the same as she? Was he too blind to see and understand or would he ever admit it? She was sick to her stomach with anxiety, *What will Fred do when he realizes what is happening.*

What should she do? What could she do? She decided to do nothing, say nothing, and let the issue ride.

While Donna waited for Kyle to return to the truck for the ride back to reception, she watched what he was doing. Why was somebody who was *just* a friend, spending so much time saying goodbye? The thought crossed her mind, if Kyle was a friend of Carl's and just a friend, why would her death and burial mean so much to him? A friend wouldn't take this much time saying goodbye to a friend's mother. All at once it hit her, *Oh my God, could he be Carl?* Her mind went into a whirl. How could this gravelly voiced, scarred person ever be Carl? Impossible! Suddenly she remembered Connie telling her several times she felt sure Kyle hadn't been honest and commented several times something wasn't right. Could he be Carl? Supposedly Carl was MIA, but could it be possible he returned to the States and the Navy didn't notify the family? She looked toward the Weston's' car and wondered what they were thinking.

Carl attended the reception but didn't want to stay long, only long enough to give his condolences to Connie, JoAnn, Fred, and the boys. He grabbed a cup of coffee, but it was used more to mask his feeling and to cover his facial expressions. He thanked Donna for coming and sitting with him. As she put on her jacket in preparation to driving home, Carl asked if she was heading for home.

Donna replied, "Yes, would you like to come over?"

"Um, yeah, I'd like that," replied Carl.

As they both walked into Donna's house, she asked if he would like anything, maybe something to drink.

More due to habit and not knowing what else to say, Carl said, "Coffee would be fine." He wasn't in the mood to return to the ranch, though feeling solitude would probably be the best antidote for his grief. On the other hand, he liked Donna's company and wanted to spend some time with her. Hell, she was the closest thing he had for a friend and couldn't explain or justify why he felt the way he did. He just needed a friend today.

11

IN A PICKLE

Donna went in, put some coffee on, and returned to the living room. She told Kyle her sister-in-law was watching Sharon, so she didn't have to dash over right away to get her. Donna wanted to ask him so many questions but didn't know what or how to broach the topics. It was quite warm, so she invited him out to the back porch where she had chairs in the shade.

Carl was quiet, so Donna left him to his thoughts, and when the coffee was ready, she got up and went to get it. Carl followed her into the house and wandered into the living room. She followed him in and watched him look at some of her family pictures.

He was looking at a picture of Sharon and commented, "Her pigtails make her look like you did." Carl knew he had said too much. He tried to hide it and act as if nothing took place but he wasn't that lucky.

Donna turned in shock and exclaimed, "Carl?"

Carl knew his cover was blown and didn't know what to say. In fact, he didn't say a word; it was as if the world stood still.

Donna demanded, "Carl, why?"

Once he came to his senses, he said, "It's a long story. Let's have some coffee and I'll tell you."

Once they each got a cup of coffee and got seated on the porch, Carl gave her a long sad look and asked, "Have you ever read *The Iliad* or *Ulysses,* by Homer? Agamemnon was the high king of Mycenae and he spent ten years fighting and conquering Troy. He took the king of Troy's daughter, Cassandra, as his slave. He spent ten years returning to his home, and during that time, fathered two children by Cassandra. He arrived back in Mycenae with all the fanfare a king might have. It wasn't the homecoming he expected because he discovered his wife was living with another man, and shortly after his arrival, she chopped his head off with an ax. She went on to murder Cassandra and her two children.

"Ulysses was also gone for the ten years of the war and spent ten more years exploring the Mediterranean Sea. During this time, his wife, Penelope had many suitors. They tried to convince her that her husband was dead or he would have already returned. She promised the suitors she would marry whoever could shoot Ulysses' bow as well as he did, and as soon as she finished weaving a burial shroud for Ulysses' father. Every night, she undid the weaving she had done during the day. Rather than coming home with fanfare, Ulysses returned after a shipwreck and appeared as a beggar. After his best friend provided him with clothes, he joined the suitors and approached Penelope as such. He took his turn and using the bow, made the perfect shot, turned, and killed every one of the suitors. He didn't have to say a word; Penelope knew he was her husband.

"I couldn't see visiting the main ranch house for one minute knowing I'd be as welcome as the plague, much like Agamemnon. "By following Ulysses' example, I slipped in the back door and avoided the storm."

Donna didn't know what to say, knowing darn well Carl was right and it was exactly what Connie wanted to avoid. Donna in the meantime was dumbfounded. She couldn't perceive the boy she liked to swing beside was right here, looking nothing like he did the last time she saw him. What a difference; what had happened?

Carl went on, "By doing it this way, I bought time, time in which I've made good on the ranch and haven't been thrown off yet. The longer I'm there, the harder it is to throw me off. Look at it this way: I've been hired to stay there and repair the place and the equipment. There's one thing I want to ask you though; please don't tell Connie."

Donna replied, "I'm her friend, and you're putting me in a pickle."

All Carl could say was, "Please," but shook his head in agreement and said, "In a pickle. I understand."

Carl had gotten incredibly quiet, so she was hoping she hadn't pried too much. His being quiet made her uneasy so she said, "I'm asking all the questions, it's your turn now." as she tried to entice him into talking again.

After an awkward silence, Carl asked Donna a couple of questions and felt awkward doing so. To him, whatever had taken place didn't matter; it was where they went from this point on that mattered. Carl knew Donna had Sharon and there had obviously been a previous marriage, but so what, it didn't matter to him. It wasn't important. His own past wasn't great and now moving on in the shape he was in, he'd be lucky to ever find a woman who would want him.

Donna finally asked Carl the nagging question she'd been dying to ask, "What happened to you Carl? Your face, you limp now, and your voice?"

Carl was quiet for some minutes and finally reiterated the ambush, the patrol boat crash, being blasted out of the boat, and subsequently being captured.

Donna asked, "What happened to your voice?"

Carl told her his vocal cords got damaged in the prison camp. He wasn't sure what happened, but when they were ambushed, the patrol boat's crew was killed, the boat hit the riverbank, and he wasn't sure what took place. The only thing he was aware of was being pulled from the water. While wishing he could lie down, he was forced to hike miles while his body ached all over, especially his face. The scars came from being blasted from the boat. My voice got messed up while in the prison camp. Carl said, "If I didn't give Charlie the information they asked for, they beat the crap out of me." He gave a small smirk. "That took place on more than one occasion, and when I crapped my pants, they could smell it and beat me some more, for stinking up the place. Between screaming because of the beatings, they hit me in the throat several times and something must have happened. My voice has never been the same. Sometimes after the beatings, they would dump me in the hole."

"What hole?" Donna asked.

"They had a solitary confinement hole with a steel plate cover. The hole wasn't long enough to lie in and it wasn't tall enough to sit up in. During the day the steel plate cover would get hotter than blazes." He paused. "I'm spilling information like an old rusty bucket spilling water."

Both Carl and Donna sat quietly for a long time after his comments.

The porch was small with the chairs arranged side by side. While sitting so close during their discussion, Carl reached over and lightly put his hand on Donna's hand.

Donna didn't move for a few minutes, but when she did, she took his hand in hers and gave him a squeeze while silent tears ran down her cheeks. In her mind she saw the boy she remembered on the swing, the boy who saved her brother, the boy she liked so many years ago. At the same time, she felt those butterflies and was happy he was sitting beside her.

It was getting late, and Donna said she'd have to go get Sharon.

Carl stood and was going to leave, but in his mind, didn't want to leave. He was self-conscious and didn't want to be too forward, but asked, "Can I see you again sometime?"

The fact he asked made her day and she said yes. "Do you want to come in sometime or what? I can't drive out anytime because the gate is locked," she said as she laughed a bit.

Carl didn't like the gate being a deterrent for Donna, but on the other hand, it assured him of his privacy. He hated the idea of strangers being able to access his home. He generally liked the solitude but Donna was different.

He definitely wanted to see her again. "If you don't mind, I'll come in; you've been to my place a lot."

FRED WAS in a foul mood because of the occasion but seeing Kyle at the memorial service and at the interment set him off. That guy had no business pushing his nose into the family's business.

Connie wanted to tell him, "He might be your cousin Carl," but couldn't, he'd never accept it, but now, she was fairly sure he wasn't Kyle. *But why? Why would Carl do such a thing? What should she do now?* Her head was spinning with worry and fear. *What would Fred do? What would happen if Kyle was Carl? Oh God, he can't t be, he just couldn't be.* She would have to talk to Kyle, but would he admit to being Carl? *What if he is Kyle? Oh my, what am I to do?*

12

THE CONFESSION

Several days later, Donna got a call from Connie. Connie sounded worried and deplored, "I need to talk to you, can I see later today?"

"Yes, let's talk this evening," commented Donna.

Connie was waiting for Donna when she got home from work. Donna invited her into the house and asked if she'd like something to drink. Connie said anything would be fine and started asking Donna about Kyle's actions at the cemetery. Connie went on, "He acted like he lost his mother or something. That's not how a friend of a friend acts. I'm sure Kyle isn't who he tells us he is. What do you think?"

Donna felt between a rock and a hard spot, so she didn't respond.

Connie rambled on, "It's as if he's Carl, but that's

impossible. How could that ever happen? So who is he and what is he? None of this makes sense. I can't believe he was a friend of Carl's like he says, but what other explanation is there? He seems to like you. You've become friends, haven't you?"

Donna looked at Connie and invited her to the back porch where they could sit in the shade. Once seated she said, "Connie, this is hard and it's a long story, but Kyle is Carl." Connie, mortified, turned and faced Donna, "No, he can't be. How can this be, Carl's MIA?"

Donna reiterated, "No, he's not, believe me. I tell you this as your friend."

Connie demanded, "How do you know?"

"We had a long talk after the service and he told me. Connie, believe me."

Connie, white with shock exclaimed, "Oh God, wait till Fred finds out."

Donna suggested, "Don't tell him. Let him find out on his own."

Connie asked, "Why did he do this? Why did he come back? What happened to him over there?"

"It's a long story, Connie, but he ran out of options. He probably wouldn't have come back, but homelessness wasn't a good option."

"Oh my, I don't know what I'm going to do, I just don't."

Donna once more suggested, “Don’t broach the topic with Fred and let him find out on his own.”

“Donna, are you sure? He doesn’t look or talk like Carl, so is Kyle trying to pull something on us?”

“Connie, he’s Carl, believe me.”

Connie was visibly shaken and Donna could certainly understand why. She was concerned for her friend, but at the same time, felt guilty for divulging Carl’s secret. The problem was, they were bound to find out sooner or later, this realization helped her justify her telling Connie. One thing she did add was the fact he had been a prisoner of war and had his vocal cords damaged while in the prison camp. She didn’t want to get into specifics, but she at least wanted Connie to know his path hadn’t been an easy one. Donna also added, “You know, he’s not a bad person; he saved my brother from drowning in the river back when they were in high school.”

Friday evening Carl knocked on Donna’s door. Sharon answered the door and while letting him in and yelled to her mother, “Kyle’s here and he’s going to read a book to me.”

Donna walked into the living room and greeted Carl as Sharon skipped to the bookshelf, her pigtails bouncing wildly. While Sharon was picking a book, Donna informed Sharon his real name is Carl and added, “We'll call him Carl from now on.” She also added, “I don’t believe Carl came by to read to you." but by that time, Sharon had her book and with a sly smile said, "Yes he did," as she handed the book to Carl.

Carl grabbed Sharon with one arm and flew her through the air and placed her on the couch, Sharon squealing all the way. Sharon liked the way he made different voices with each character. He was so much fun. To Carl, it was so awkward, but seeing how fast childhood slips by--and war leaves childhood like a rogue storm leaves a ship smashed on a rocky shore--these moments were vital, awkward, but important. For him it was a moment he could see what he'd like to be.

Finishing the book, he gave it back to Sharon and went to the kitchen where Donna was finishing the dinner dishes. She invited him to the back porch where it was cooler and told him of Connie's visit and the fact she had informed Connie of Carl's real identity. She added, "I hope you're not angry, but she was so upset and she is a friend."

Donna expected Carl to get angry but he sat there and nodded his head in agreement. He commented, "She'd figure it out sometime anyway." Carl took her hand in his and remarked, "It's okay. Like you said, I put you in a pickle."

They both chuckled. Donna was so happy he was understanding and not angry with her. She also realized he knew what a friend was and didn't expect anything less.

Donna informed him she didn't have any coffee on but asked if he would like something cold.

"That would be fine," he said as he followed her into the kitchen.

As she started to reach for a couple of glasses on a shelf, Carl was looking at her slender body with wonderment. The way she eased into his life was a puzzle he wasn't expecting. Her gentleness and understanding reeled at his heart. She caught him; that was for sure. He couldn't stop thinking about her.

He stepped closer to her with butterflies in his belly but with sheer determination steadied himself as he clasped her hands in his. He held her hands for a long moment. His eyes spoke volumes of how he felt. He stood above her and, finally, pulled her close to him, cupping her girlish face in his scarred and calloused hands, making her feel cute and pretty. As their lips touched the first time it was a peck, but the second and the third times, much longer. Happiness blindsided him; the war was ten lifetimes ago.

Their fourth kiss was interrupted by Sharon's loud voice, "Mom!" as she walked into the room.

Donna was a bit surprised and incredibly happy at the same time. Being brought back to reality, Donna got them both a glass of iced tea and while holding their drinks, they walked hand in hand to the back porch.

Donna's mind was running wild as she realized how Carl felt about her. She was so happy she didn't know what to say and decided she'd leave it up to Carl.

Carl was ready to grab her again and hug her for as long as forever but since they took their seats, didn't want to push his luck. Those kisses they shared in the kitchen were sheer ecstasy in his mind. Nothing on this earth compared to the feeling he had while holding and kissing her.

A number of minutes went by, and they both finally spoke at the same time saying, "You know I…" and both stopped and looked at each other.

Another awkward moment went by and Donna said, "You first."

Carl responded with, "I want you know that I want to hold you for the rest of my life."

"Nothing would make me happier," Donna's reply.

Carl asked, "Donna, how do you think Sharon will feel about you and me?"

Donna replied, "She won't mind. She likes being with you, you know, at the ranch and all. She sure enjoyed your reading to her."

Small talk continued and Donna asked if he got the tractor running yet.

"Yes, but it isn't running like it should. I'm going to have to pull it apart again."

"Have you started on the hay truck?"

"No, I don't want two big jobs going at the same time. Besides, if Fred drops by and sees nothing but piles of parts, I'd be in trouble."

"Why did you get expelled from school?" Donna asked.

"One more fight, but since it took place in the classroom, the bad apple was thrown out."

"What was the fight over?"

Carl replied, "I don't remember." Carl didn't want to go into that tale. Besides, his uncle wailed the holy hell out of him when he got home. Two weeks later they shipped him off to the academy. It's a great way to get rid of a problem child. When he graduated, he didn't have any money, couldn't get a job, so he joined the Navy. At least they trained him to repair engines. All would have been fine if they hadn't transferred him to the patrol boats. Changing the subject, Carl asked, "How did you and Connie become friends?"

Donna explained how they met while she was volunteering at the county fair. "I always like to help at the fair, and Connie always had her boys with her, so Sharon and the boys would hang out together. They sort of became her babysitters while at the fair. Once the fair started, Connie's boys always showed animals, so I had to look after Sharon while the exhibits actually opened, but she always liked to see the animals they were showing. We always attended the judging when the boys were showing too. In a way, I suppose we became close because of our children. I always looked forward to the fair because it's the only time we are able see each other. I worked at the school, and Connie was always on the ranch. Our lives were so different, if it wasn't for the fair and the kids, we'd never have met much less become friends."

"Once I got married and had Sharon, I had to work to help make ends meet and lost contact with most of my high school friends. So getting together with Connie at the annual fair was a real treat. Connie and the boys always attended because they showed cows, pigs, or goats, so they had to be at the showings and also being judged. Naturally Sharon couldn't miss those events either. She was their biggest fan, much like brothers and sister. I believe your arrival pushed Connie into a corner and she needed a friend to confide in, that's why we've recently seen more of each other."

Carl liked hearing Donna tell of her life but finally had to excuse himself and head for home. As he got ready to leave, he commented, "Oh, I had keys made so you can open the gate whenever you wish," and gave Donna a key to the gate.

The following weekend, Donna and Sharon visited Carl.

Sharon pestered her mom all week till Donna told her they would visit Carl on the weekend. Actually, Donna liked seeing Carl and now she had a key to the gate; so Sharon was providing the extra push.

They weren't in the house long before Sharon went to the back door and didn't see the toys she had left in the garden. "Where's my toys?" she asked loudly.

Sharon wanted to play in the tilled up garden where the soil was easy to dig.

Carl went to the door, stepped out, and commented, "Look in the little tool shed." As he pointed to a doghouse-sized shed he built. Sharon ran over and reached inside, there she found a wheelbarrow, a shovel, and a rake, all little girl-sized, and her bucket and digging can.

"Wow, are they mine?" she asked.

"Yes, and that's where they go when you're finished playing with them." instructed Carl.

Carl smiled to himself knowing his free ranging chickens and the recently acquired kittens he got earlier in the week would help keep snakes and rodents out of the toy shed. Barn cats were his plan for the kittens. He wondered where they were since Sharon hadn't found them yet. He knew she'd go nuts with excitement when she discovered them.

Donna was standing beside Carl being curious about what had happened to the toys also. It made her smile knowing Carl had made the wheelbarrow, the little shed, and purchased the little gardening tools for Sharon. A half hour later Sharon, squealing with delight, came in with the kittens in her arms.

CONNIE WAS GOING through the billings and saw the property taxes arrived. As she opened the envelope and read the billing, she got concerned because the taxes were greatly reduced from what they had always been. This confused her so she brought it to Fred's attention.

Fred looked at it and said, "We'll have to go to the county courthouse to find out what mistake the county has made now. There has to be some mistake."

Connie grumbled, "That will eat the better part of a day."

The next day they drove into Deer Lodge and visited the county auditor. Fred pointed out the mistake and the clerk looked up the tax records. The clerk informed Fred the taxes were correct and the billing covered the parcels listed. Fred asked to see a map, it was clear to him the billing covered the lower half of the ranch. Fred brought this to the clerk's attention and was informed that the other parcels, the other half of the ranch was owned by somebody else.

Fred was getting irritated and demanded, "And just *who* owns them?"

The clerk looked up the information and replied, "Carl Weston owns them."

Fred's face got red, his anger boiled over, "That's impossible, when did this take place?" he demanded.

The clerk looked at the dates and when informed, Fred realized it as one month before his mother died. Fred, instantly angry thought, *What in the hell has Mother done?* All he could say was to Connie, "Let's go."

As Fred slammed the car door, turned to Connie, and asked, "Did you know about this?"

"No" and she got no farther.

Fred interrupted her by shouting in her face, "Did you know Mom gave him the title to our land?"

Oncc more she said, "No." To say the least, she was as shocked as Fred.

Fred demanded, "Is that guy Kyle trying to pull a fast one? Does he think he can pull this off? You say you didn't know; well your friend Donna sure as hell knew. Some friend she is." His voice rose to a shout. "Was she in on this?"

All Connie could think was, Oh God, this is what I was afraid would happen.

Fred drove straight to the upper ranch to the cabin. Seething with anger, he bounded up onto the porch and hammered on the door with his fist. Carl answered the door and stepped onto the porch as Fred demanded, "What kind of game are you trying to pull? This is my land and you're not going to squat on it." He saw Donna and told her, 'Why don't you leave, this isn't any business of yours, or is it?"

Carl tried to explain the fact he had clear title and therefore owned the upper range lands. If Fred would calm down and listen, he could pay Carl's lawyer a visit and an equitable price could be arrived at for the continued use of the upper range. Carl said he wasn't trying to damage the ranch and hoped this hiccup could be overcome. There wasn't any reason the cattle couldn't use the upper range; it would have to carry a cost now. The ranch would run like a partnership, both costs and income would be shared by both parties. In other words, both parties would share in the profits of the ranch.

Sharon, hearing the commotion, came out from the back of the house and shyly stood behind Carl and her mother.

Fred stepped closer to Carl and shouted, "You think

you can get away with this but you're wrong. I'll see you off this ranch, if I have to get the sheriff to haul you off."

Carl replied, "Why don't you just shut your gob and leave? Because I have the title and you know it."

"Dammit Carl, why don't you go back to where you came from? You've lied about who you are and now you think you own the place."

Hearing "go back to where you came from," made Carl see the war and the shit storm it was, so he stood his ground and seethed.

Fred shouted, "You were nothing but trouble, and I've lived with enough of your crap."

Carl replied, "I know we never got along as kids, but that was when we were kids. Everything is different now; the least we can do is get along. The ranch depends on us working as a family. I didn't come here to take anything from you. We have to live with your mother's wishes."

Fred's anger flashed red; he grabbed a fistful of Carl's shirt front, but lacking the training Carl had, found himself lying on the ground. Carl didn't slug him but twisted him and dumped him on the ground.

"No!" Connie screamed with tears in her eyes.

Carl could feel his adrenaline climbing and didn't want this to escalate. He wasn't sure what he might do, but it wouldn't be pretty. He hated having to do this to his cousin but this had to end. Fred had to know the land was his and he was going to stay on it. Carl stepped away so Fred could get up.

As Fred walked back to his car, he screamed, "We'll see about this! I have a lawyer you know!" Before he got into the car, he had to have the last word. "Your days on this ranch are numbered. The sheriff will be coming to take you off, just wait and see!"

On the drive home, he ranted at Connie for not seeing what had happened right before her eyes. "Your friend isn't much of a friend to crap on you--us--this way."

Connie hated seeing Fred in these raging moods and cried most of the way home. She tried to explain that Donna was a good friend and didn't deserve the trash he was saying.

"Yes," Fred said, "she's a good friend. She's living with him, and you call her a good friend?"

"They're not living together. She lives in town on Alder Street."

Fred explained his plan. He would stop paying Carl the maintenance salary he'd been paying him, then Carl wouldn't be able to afford the taxes on the land. Carl would be forced to sell it to Fred.

Connie pointed out that if he couldn't pay the taxes, Carl might find a higher bidder and the land would be lost to the family. "We'd be sunk if that ever took place. He said he wanted to work with us, but since you're being so unreasonable, he wants us to work through his lawyer. Don't let your anger get the better of you and do something rash."

Carl stayed rooted where he was on the porch as Fred and Connie drove away. Another sleepless night of flashbacks was on his mind knowing it was this confrontation he had tried so hard to avoid. Donna stepped closer to him and while taking his hand, gave it a squeeze. Carl pulled her close and hugged her while she buried her face against his neck and returned his hug.

Sharon walked from the corner of the house where she had been standing and while approaching them said in a timid voice, "That man scared me."

Carl reached out and pulled her into a tight hug against her mother and him while telling her, "Nobody will ever hurt you, if I can help it."

Carl's word "ever" put Donna's mind in a whirl, *What did he say? Was he saying what I think? Is he telling me how he feels about the two of us? Does he mean what he told Sharon or was he only trying to comfort her for the moment?* While the three of them stood there in the threesome hug, Donna loved the feeling yet couldn't break her sense of concern, what would a future with Carl be, and was it what she wanted or needed? *If he was willing to do anything for Sharon's safety, was he also telling her he would do the same for her?*

The following evening, Connie stopped by Donna's house to talk. She asked Donna, "Did you know Carl had the title to the land?"

"No, I was under the impression Carl was getting paid for maintaining the area."

Connie explained, "He was up until yesterday. I'm sorry Fred was so rude to you yesterday. I'm sure you're not surprised at Fred's anger though; this has all been so stressful. I trust you won't let it come between us. I'd hate to lose your friendship over this."

"I understand completely and no, it won't affect our friendship. Your friendship is too precious to me." replied Donna while feeling sorry for Connie.

13

REMINISCING

Eventually Fred and Connie visited the lawyer and an equitable system was agreed upon where both parties were basically partners and the ranch's cattle would use both ranges. This arrangement allowed Fred and Connie to run the ranch, continue living as they had, and enjoy their lives. It also allowed Carl to continue living on the upper range, afford the taxes and maintenance, and enjoy his life.

DONNA DIDN'T OFTEN EAT at the café, but on this occasion, Sharon was at a friend's house for a sleepover so she decided to not have to fix anything for herself. While eating, she overheard a couple of men eating at the counter remarked, "I hear there's one of those Vietnam veterans living on the Weston ranch."

The other man also commented, "Yes, that's what I heard too, and he keeps the gate locked so nobody can get in..."

Donna couldn't help but wonder why there was animosity in their discussion. The gate was always locked; it had nothing to do with Carl's being there. Granted, he liked solitude and privacy, but like all ranches, it's a common practice to keep all gates locked. There isn't a ranch in the county that doesn't have their gates locked. The Weston ranch wasn't any different.

The next day Donna saw the headlines in the local newspaper: "Vietnam Veteran Usurps Ranch from Long-Time Owner." As she glanced through the article, she read where the reporter stated Carl refused to be interviewed. The reporter went on to explain how Carl stayed on the ranch behind a locked gate, making it sound like he was hiding from the reporter. Donna knew the gate was always locked so it had nothing to do with the reporter.

The next time she saw Carl, she asked him if he'd seen the article. Carl said he had and added, "The reporter came by the auto shop. After shaking hands with him using my greasy dirty hands, I informed him I was working by the hour and he wasn't paying my wages. I also told him customers and the public are not welcome in the work area of the shop. It wouldn't matter what I said, they would print what they liked and it wouldn't be in my favor. So, why say anything at all?"

Donna understood exactly how Carl felt and agreed with him.

Several weeks later, Donna visited the ranch to see Carl, since she now had a key to the ranch gate and Sharon was at a Bible camp for the weekend. Carl was preparing the garden for another season and Donna wanted to help him. By the time she arrived, it was time to start the planting. It took all day, so Carl suggested they go into town for dinner, his treat. Granted, they weren't dressed for a date, but it was almost as if it was a date. They each drove their own vehicles into town so they didn't have to go back and get Donna's car later. They both appreciated not having to take time to fix dinner and Carl enjoyed his time with her.

Donna was also enjoying her time with Carl and didn't want the evening to end, so after they ate, she asked, "Would you like to come over to the house for a while?"

"Sure, that would be great." responded Carl.

Once they got to Donna's she put on some coffee and quickly changed into cleaner clothes. When the coffee was ready, they filled their cups and went out on the back porch to sit in the warm evening air. They both sat and sipped their coffee there for a while, neither one of them speaking for a quite few minutes. Each one wanted to speak but couldn't find the words or the topic. It was awkward, and Donna knew most men like to reminisce about their old school days and their sports. Though as far as she could recall, Carl didn't play on any of the team sports. Donna also knew from her conversations with Connie he'd been in enough trouble for two kids but she couldn't help remembering what her brother had told her.

Donna finally said after a hesitating breath, "My brother told me you rescued him from the river one time. He also said you were the only person who tried to help him."

"Yeah, I caught holy hell for going swimming in the river too. I hadn't gone in till your brother needed help. So that was your brother? Small world, huh."

Donna added, "Yeah, Steve caught holy hell too. He never did tell Mom and Dad he nearly drowned. Why weren't you ever on any of the teams?" Donna asked.

"Most of the jocks didn't like me, and I suppose the feeling was mutual," He told her. Carl didn't like the way this was going but wasn't sure how to change the conversation. He didn't like discussing unhappy bygones, much less people who might be friends or relatives to whoever he was talking to.

Donna mentioned she liked to swing with him when

they were in grade school. The trouble was, he was more interested in seeing how high he could go.

Carl said, "So many of the other boys were so much better than me at sports, but I was always able to outdo them on the swings. You know, that picture of your Sharon reminded me of the little girl who used to always be on the swings. Even her pigtails are the same. But what the hell, that was grade school."

Donna couldn't help feeling the butterflies in her stomach with his comment. He actually remembered her. "Did you go to the prom?" she asked.

"No, all the girls wanted to go with the cool, popular guys."

"Did you ask any of the girls in your class to the prom?" Donna wanted to know.

"No, they wouldn't give me the time of day. I wasn't popular or on the team. Besides, I beat every one of those guy's butts, so in those girl's eyes, I was a cur dog. They wouldn't so much as look at me. Hell, the closest they would come near me was if they had to sit next to me in a class," replied Carl.

"Why did you do that?" Donna asked.

"Because they would take me on two or three at a time, but if I could get each one alone, they paid dearly for it. Damn though, I'd catch holy hell once my uncle found out about it."

Donna commented, "I know I was a year younger than you, but did you ever think of asking me out?"

Carl was quiet for a few minutes before answering, "Yeah, but I guess I chickened out. Sounds dumb now, but you know, I didn't think you'd want to go with me."

Donna was shocked and replied, "You beat up every football player on the team and you were afraid to ask me out!"

Sheepishly, Carl replied, "Yeah, something like that, I guess."

Donna was speechless for a few minutes. She couldn't imagine Carl being afraid of anything, especially after his being a prisoner of war and his escape. Donna added, "You got expelled from the school, so your folks--your uncle--sent you to a military academy. Did you like it there?"

Carl replied, "Not really, but I got along. I learned to keep my mouth shut. That way people don't know what you're thinking. I could take care of myself. When I graduated, I didn't plan on returning home so I joined the Navy."

Donna continued, "Why did they expel you?"

"One too many fights, why?" asked Carl.

Donna replied, "I understood all your fights were all off the school grounds."

After a brief pause, Carl commented, "The last fight

took place in the classroom. Do you remember Susan Townberger?"

"Yes," replied Donna, "she works at the café now."

Carl continued, "She wasn't popular, nor was she the prettiest girl in the class. Anyway, before class started, Deric, one of the football team jocks, grabbed her purse and ran around the room with it. Susan tried to get her purse back and chased him. The class was laughing and yelling, 'Go Deric, go Deric.' On his second time around the classroom, and crossing in front of the class, he dumped everything out of her purse and it flew all over the floor. She had female stuff and a spare pair of panties in her purse along with everything else girls keep in there. Can you imagine how humiliated she was having the whole class laughing at her and now, her private stuff was all over the floor? The last thing in the world a teen girl wants is for any boy much less the whole class to see is her private stuff."

"Anyway, Deric came running past my desk, and I jumped up, grabbed his arm, jerked him around, and my fist caught him right in the nose. Blood flew everywhere, and he hit the floor screaming. I didn't know it at the time, but I broke his arm and nose. I knew I'd be in trouble so I walked to the front of the room and started helping Susan pick up her stuff. Mr. Conner walked into the room. I can still hear him yell, 'Carl, get to the office, now!' When I gave Susan what I had picked up, her expression screamed, *how dare you touch my stuff? I hate you*. That's all the thanks I got."

"While I was picking up Susan's stuff and on my way out of the room, the girls were yelling 'Carl love's Susan.' I've often wondered how humiliated Susan felt. Anyway, two weeks later I was attending the military academy."

"What was it like?" Donna asked.

"Just another school except the students were from families that didn't want their brats at home, families with kids who had one foot in jail, or families willing to send their sons away to dodge the responsibility of having to marry some gal they had gotten pregnant."

What Carl didn't tell her was a particular incident while he was in second or third grade. He was playing on the merry-go-round with a bunch of his classmates, and as the recess bell rang, they pushed him off. While he was rolling on the ground, they all got off and ran back to class laughing and jeering at him. While getting off the ground and brushing off his scraped hands, knees, and elbows, he was so angry, he lashed out at the first person he saw. Susan Townberger was sitting on a swing nearby so he walked over to her and yanked one of her braids as hard as he could. While walking back to class, he realized what a terrible thing to do since she hadn't been part of the merry-go-round group. It wasn't a proud moment in his life; her scream and her tear streaked face never left his memory. Nope, that wasn't something he would ever talk about.

From that day forward, he never took his frustrations out on anybody who didn't deserve it. Granted, later in middle school and high school, the boys discovered the only way they could best him was to gang up on him. That or steal his homework so he wouldn't be able to turn it in. The kids who picked on him usually made sure they were never alone in his presence because when he did encounter them alone, vengeance was his and they paid dearly in blood and tears.

All that childhood crap ended the day he joined the Navy. There he was a team member and everybody depended on each other. On the PBR, they depended on him to keep the twin diesels running at their best. He also kept them squeaky clean so he could see any problems if they developed. The other crewmen depended on his engines as he depended on the two gunners mates with the machine guns and the skipper. Poor performance was never an issue because each crewman's life was at stake.

Carl had gotten noticeably quiet, so Donna was hoping she hadn't pried too much. His being quiet made her uneasy so she said, "I'm asking all the questions; it's your turn now."

Carl asked a few questions concerning Donna's earlier

life, including why she was always volunteering at the county fair. After Donna explained how much she like to work at the fair and how much Sharon enjoyed the fair, she asked Carl about his plans for the ranch. Carl explained he never planned on leaving, and that was the reason for repairing everything. He also put in the large garden because he was short of money, and it was the easiest way to assure himself of always having food. Besides, what else did he have to do other than working part time at the auto shop?

As Donna went to refill their coffee cups, Carl got up and followed her into the kitchen. Standing beside Donna, he put his cup on the counter, he wanted to put his arms around her but he sure didn't want to do anything that might hurt their friendship. He valued their relationship beyond words. Before Donna reached for the coffee pot, Carl put his arms around her. Carl wasn't sure what or how but before he knew it, their lips met and once again kissed each other. His mind went crazy and he couldn't believe this was happening. Donna was a bit surprised but turned so they could both embrace and she wasn't sure who kissed who but it all happened at once, they were kissing each other. Carl was the first to sheepishly remember they were going to refill their coffee cups and released Donna, they refilled their cups and returned to the back porch.

Donna was so happy, she felt like she was walking on air. She couldn't help thinking; *finally, it took him long enough.* She liked him and wanted to spend time with him but he sure didn't make it easy.

Carl's brain was whirling; Donna didn't say anything so he wondered what she was thinking or how she felt. He sure hoped he hadn't poked a wrench in their relationship. She did kiss him back, so he supposed she didn't mind. While these thoughts were going through his mind, he took her hand. *Damn, I like her. Probably more than I should, too.*

He'd never felt this way about a girl so had no idea how to approach the situation. He couldn't help noticing she was still holding his hand so that was a good sign.

On the following Saturday afternoon Donna was having coffee with one of the school employees at the cafe and discussing the upcoming end-of-year school program. As she started to leave and while standing near the door by the cash register waiting to pay her bill, she overheard two men sitting at a nearby table.

"I heard that crazy vet out on the Weston land swindled Fred out of his ranch. There was an article in the newspaper about it too."

The second man commented, "How did that happen?"

"I don't know," replied the first. "All I know is he works part time at the auto shop and other than that, he never leaves the ranch."

"Has Fred asked the sheriff to evict the nut?"

"I don't know, but half those guys who came back from Vietnam are half-crazy."

By this time Donna's coffee tasted like bitter acid and all she wanted to do was go home. On her way home, Donna wondered if Carl knew what some people thought of him.

SEVERAL DAYS later Carl stopped by Donna's house after work. Business was booming at the auto shop, so, the manager didn't mind if Carl worked longer hours than normal.

After they had chatted awhile, Donna asked him, "Carl, have you ever considered taking classes at a community college? You could do it with your GI benefits."

Carl explained, "The GI benefits needed to be started within ten years of getting out of the service. I'm still listed as MIA, and ten years have gone by. Maybe someday the government will change it but for now, I can't access that resource. I know ranching and can repair most stuff, so I'm happy where I'm at."

Donna timidly added, "The other day I overheard some people talking, and their discussion wasn't being kind concerning you and other veterans."

Carl responded, "I suppose we think a little different than they do. They would think differently too if they saw their friends get shot or had the shit beat out of them in a prison camp. I also know many of the vets have drug problems, but who wouldn't in their shoes? I'm one of the lucky ones; my drug habit is caffeine; I don't live without it."

He took a deep breath, "During those years I was working my way from Cambodia and Singapore to America, I'd have never made it if I was doing drugs. I had to keep my head on straight and work like a dog. People have no idea how hard it is to ingratiate oneself to somebody who couldn't care less if you lived or died. I had to survive and work with people I couldn't talk to because I didn't speak their language, yet I had to learn how to convince them I could fix their boat engines and help them fish. I worked nearly a year with the first fisherman that helped me and then I spent two years with a Chinese woman and her child helping her operate her bum boat. We did everything from sell stuff and make deliveries. If a freighter was in port, we would go alongside and sell fish, vegetables, clothing, jewelry, and sometimes stuff people weren't supposed to have. Those foreign ships were our rice bowl--to you that would be our bread and butter. One time we delivered firearms to a ship. Chi Lou Mei would have been imprisoned for the rest of her life if we'd have gotten caught. She did the talking and I did the work and never opened my mouth. I could keep her old boat's engine going and that's all she cared about. That's all either one of us cared about. She's the one who finally got me to Singapore. She's the one who hooked me up with the Chinese fellow who finally got me on the freighter to Manila and San Francisco."

He rubbed his hands through his hair and then said, "Am I crazy? Maybe, but those cupcakes you overheard couldn't hold a candle to Chi Lou Mei and the things we did to survive. It's the cupcakes who call us all the bad names; all the while it was their government that sent us over there to do their thankless job. On top of that, they wouldn't let us win, so in either case, we're the rotten dregs of humanity in their eyes. If you ever look closely, you'll see every one of those cupcakes come from well-to-do, middle class families. The most difficult thing they ever did was get through high school and college. They didn't have to go since they had the means to stay in college and beat the draft. Isn't it nice to call those who got their hands dirty over there crazy or murderers while they got to stay home and get an education so they could be years ahead of us in the job market?" Trying to change the subject, Carl added, "Ah, to hell with it, I can match them any day, ranching."

THAT NIGHT CARL woke after reliving the day he ended up living with Chi Lou Mei. They were in some small port in South Vietnam when the fisherman he was working with left for some errands. A Chinese lady on a small junk was having engine trouble, so Carl stepped on board her boat and took one look at her engine and after several minutes, got it running for her. In the meantime, a port official boarded her boat and started arguing with the lady. During the altercation, the official tripped, fell overboard, got bitten by a brown sea snake, and died within minutes. The police visited the boat, retrieved the body, and interrogated the woman. Carl tried to leave the boat but wasn't allowed to since he was regarded as part of the crime. Hours later, nothing had been resolved because the lady said the man tripped and fell, and no, she didn't push him. She also showed the police how the port official stubbed his foot on the deck fitting. Carl would only grunt so they couldn't discover he only knew English and was an undocumented person. Carl was frightened as hell knowing he was about to be imprisoned. The police finally instructed the lady to leave port and never return. As soon as they disembarked, she started the engine and they left port. Carl had no idea where she was going, and now he was a captive on board her boat.

He woke and like after any of his bad dreams, he, got dressed, and went to the kitchen. He wouldn't sleep--hell, he didn't want to sleep and have that dream again--so he fixed coffee and sat out on the front porch.

LATER THAT WEEK, Donna got Sharon off to bed and while getting herself ready for bed, couldn't get Carl out of her mind. She understood why he got angry and it wasn't with her. People's reaction to his wanting to be secure wasn't something he could control. She also hoped she hadn't damaged their relationship when he divulged those years he never talked about. Would he treat her the same after getting so personal?

She didn't know.

She couldn't imagine having to live on a small boat for several years with somebody you couldn't talk too, much less a woman and child. That had to have been an awkward relationship and living arrangement. Yet as he described it, it was a matter of survival and the only way to get back home. She suddenly realized what he had previously told Connie about working those years on farms in California was anything but the truth. He had been slowly working his way as best he could from Cambodia to Singapore and home.

Thinking about it made her shudder.

While she was thinking about the years it took him to get back to the states, she finally understood why he was listed as MIA. He had been a prisoner of war but since his escape took place before it was liberated, he wasn't at the prison so rather than listing him as POW, the Navy listed him as MIA. Of course the Navy didn't notify the family he had returned because in their records, he was still MIA though he was actually still trying to get back home. Granted, once back, he worked on some farms long enough to be able to afford the drive back to Montana.

Donna wondered if the people were partly correct or not. Carl had changed in many respects, but at the same time, in many respects he hadn't changed. She greatly respected his tenacity; once he made up his mind, nothing was going to change it. He didn't want visitors, so he made it hard for people to access his space. Back in their school days, those who treated him like dirt usually got a dose of their own medicine back.

It hurt Donna to see how some people felt knowing Carl would do anything for those who treated him with respect. Could or should she continue her relationship with him was something she had to consider. Since he was her first love--call it puppy love or first crush--it left her with strong feelings towards him. He was always good to her and Sharon as well. Carl always made her feel safe and appreciated too. Granted, he wasn't the most talkative person, making it hard to get to know him much less know how he felt, but when he did say something, there wasn't any doubt left for misunderstandings.

Donna couldn't help remembering back and her first husband; he had been so nice to her yet turned nasty after Sharon was born. Would something like that happen with Carl? On the other hand, Carl tried to avoid all of the everyday drama so many people indulge in. Work relationships are full of politics, volunteering for the county fair had its share of politics and silly people problems. *It's no wonder Carl avoids them, it's all so unnecessary.*

One feeling Donna couldn't dispel was the wonderful feeling she got while working with Carl canning the vegetables and, of course, when he held her. The touch of his hand on hers gave her butterflies.

A WEEK later Carl was in town and decided to take Donna to dinner. This included both Donna and Sharon, so it wasn't intimate, but it was right up Carl's ally. Sharon could keep one busy answering questions, but both Donna and Carl had a chance to visit with a small amount of conversation though Carl didn't indulge in small talk and enjoyed being with Donna.

Later when he took them home, as Sharon got out of the car, Carl opened the door for Donna. They walked up to the porch; Donna let Sharon in and turned to face Carl. He put his arms around her and held her. After a good night kiss, Donna turned to open the door.

Carl couldn't help thinking how much he liked Donna. He liked being close to her so once more he put his arms around her waist and as he squeezed her tight, he said, "I wish I could hold you forever."

Donna turned and while giving him a hug and a kiss, considered it was as close as he'd ever come to saying, "I love you." She also knew he wasn't angry with her over that one evening's conversation.

14

JOANN INVESTIGATES

JoAnn was concerned about her father's ranch being usurped by Kyle, an imposter who supposedly turned out to be her uncle Carl. This was all hard to believe, so she made plans to visit the ranch and ask some questions of her own. *Why did he do it? How did he manage to get ownership of half the ranch?* Since she wasn't Fred's biological daughter, he wasn't her uncle, right?

She still had a key to the gate, so she let herself through and drove on to the ranch house. Carl answered her knock and immediately invited her in and offered coffee, which she declined, he waited to see why she stopped in.

JoAnn asked, "So what do I call you, Kyle or Carl?"

Carl replied, "Carl will do."

She thanked him for being so nice to her while they

were stranded during his first winter. His being kind didn't erase his other transgressions in her mind though. Once that uncomfortable task was done, she felt she could ask her more pressing questions.

Carl explained as best he could about his and Fred's rough and bumpy relationship. There was a clash of personalities and for whatever reason couldn't be repaired. He also explained to her how he viewed the family's attitude towards him.

Carl continued, "When my uncle--Fred's father--got the chance, he shipped me off to a military boarding school and wrote me off." Carl asked JoAnn, "How much sleep do you think any of your family lost knowing I was in Vietnam, knowing I was a POW, and later being told I was MIA?"

JoAnn wouldn't answer his question because while she knew his name, he was seldom ever spoken of at home.

CARL WENT ON, "I knew ahead of time I'd be as welcome as the plague, so why would I so much as darken your family's doorstep? I'm sure you know as well as I do, I'd have been told to leave and don't let the door hit my butt on the way out."

JoAnn was getting uncomfortable the way this

conversation was going, so she asked if he was her real uncle.

"No, but as far as I'm concerned you are my niece. I was happy to be able to attend your wedding too. Granted Fred isn't your real father, but as far as your life has gone, he's the only father you have."

Carl didn't mind JoAnn's visit and knew much of what he would tell her wouldn't correspond with Fred's views. Oh well, he couldn't help that. He had been honest and there darn well wasn't any sugar coating.

JoAnn asked how he managed to get title to half the ranch. In her mind, he cheated her family; it should belong to Fred, Bill, Mike, and her.

Carl informed her, "Aunt Carol deeded it to me." She couldn't believe it and wouldn't accept it.

"Why would she do that?" she asked.

Carl explained, "Because she knew Fred would never give me half, or for that matter, share any part of the ranch with me."

JoAnn's reply was, "But you're not part of the family."

"I was part of your family ever since I was five. You're grandma Carol was the only mother I had or knew after my parents died in the fire. Her whole world included you, Fred, me, and the ranch."

JoAnn's next question was, "Why didn't you stay in California?"

Carl instantly thought this must be a rehashed question often dished up when Fred was talking about him. He tried to answer her question concerning how difficult it was to find work and choosing to live in the cabin rather than being homeless.

JoAnn wasn't happy with most of the answers Carl gave but felt she understood the situation better. Before she left, she asked about Vietnam so he described a few of his experiences there and in the prison camp.

She was both frustrated and disappointed by the time she left the cabin. Her family suddenly losing half the ranch was disappointing. It should have all gone to Bill, Mike and her. Now half could eventually go to Sharon and she wasn't even a part of the family. *Why did her grandmother do this?* It didn't make sense.

Carl's explanation concerning the fact that Fred would never have shared any part of the ranch, the inheritance, with him didn't make sense to her because in her mind, none of it should go to him, even if he did live with them for twelve years.

According to Fred, Carl was nothing but a burden and always in trouble anyway. JoAnn knew her husband was hoping they would get a portion of the lump sum payment when it was sold. Well, at least he had a good job, so they weren't depending on anything from the ranch. JoAnn and her husband had recently moved to Deer

Lodge because of his new job. JoAnn liked living in the city and leaving ranch life behind.

She knew her husband believed the ranch would end up being sold because Bill didn't want to run it and their mother wasn't going to be able to for very many more years. Mike would probably make a hash of it if he tried so where did that leave the ranch? JoAnn stood to get a tidy sum.

15

THE CONFRONTATION

Donna was fixing dinner and Carl had entered the house just as they heard what sounded like motorcycles in the distance. Carl looked out the window and saw two ATVs and two motorcycles coming down the road towards the ranch house.

Carl's first thought was, *they either cut the gate chain or the fence to get through, so this isn't going to be good, and they are trespassing.* Carl quickly grabbed the M1 Garand from over the doorway and some ammunition while telling Donna, "You meet them on the porch and don't ever look at the woodshed. That would give me away and I don't want them to know where I'm at." With that, Carl dashed out the back door and sprinted to the woodshed where he would be able to see the front yard area.

Four men rode to the front of the house; Carl

recognized Deric Hollingsworth and Roger Wheeler but didn't know the other two fellows. Donna stepped out onto the front porch as the four were getting off their machines.

Before she could ask what they wanted, Deric asked, "Where's Carl?"

Donna replied, "Carl's not here. What do you want?"

"The hell he isn't, his pickup's still here. We want him to give the ranch back to Fred, this isn't Carl's land."

Donna commented, "It's Carl's land, and you're trespassing."

All four men started walking towards the house, and Donna got frightened but remembered: *don't look at the woodshed.* She glanced in the opposite direction. The four men noticed her glance and also looked in that direction and just as Deric stepped onto the porch.

BOOM!

They all turned to see one of the motorcycles in flames created by the tracer bullet that was fired through its gas tank. "My bike!" its owner screamed.

Carl stepped from the woodshed and said, "Looks like your bike had a short or something. Now it's time for you to get off my property. You're trespassing and not welcome. For your information, this is my legal property and you have no right to be here, much less harass my friend."

The four men saw Carl and the rifle he was holding and realized it was best to leave. The fourth man had to ride double on one of the ATVs. As they drove away, one of them shouted back, "You bastard!"

Once they were gone far enough and they couldn't create a problem, Carl walked over and gave Donna a big hug. Donna was noticeably frightened and trembling. She pointed at the burned remains of the bike and asked, "What are you going to do with that? Did you have to destroy his bike?"

Carl replied, "They had to either damage the gate or cut the fence, so it was time to take names and kick ass." Carl smiled to himself for using an old Navy expression he hadn't used since escaping the prison camp. "Since he didn't take his trash with him, I'll probably have to take it to the dump."

"What's going to happen now?"

Carl replied, "Nothing, because they were trespassing and I'll have to repair the damage they did. They didn't just drive through."

Donna added, "They scared me. Do you think that they will try to damage your truck when you're in town?"

Carl replied, "They could, but the bike was worth a hell of a lot more than my old truck. I sure wish I could have shot Deric's rig, but his was closest to the house and the people. As it was, the one I shot was close enough, and one never knows how far shrapnel might fly."

That night, once more Carl awoke after dreaming of being blasted from the patrol boat, being pulled from the water, and being taken captive. He was soaked in sweat, his heart pounding, and he knew, he'd sleep no more, so he fixed coffee and spent the night sitting on the front porch.

A WEEK later the sheriff dropped by the auto shop and asked Carl about shooting Steve Colter's bike.

Carl responded with, "I didn't shoot the bike; it had a short or something. Granted, I had a rifle because those guys cut my fence to gain access and were trespassing. They threatened my friend Donna and scared her half to death because her daughter was also in the house. They had absolutely no business cutting my fence to gain access so they could threaten us. You also have the responsibility of protecting my rights as well as theirs."

The sheriff asked where the bike was because he'd like to see it.

Carl informed him it was at the city dump. "I recognized Deric and Roger and I think one of them was Steve Colter. Who was the fourth one?"

The sheriff didn't answer the question.

THREE DAYS later the sheriff corralled Carl at the auto shop again and said, "I found the bike at the dump but couldn't find the fuel tank."

Carl responded, "I don't know what to tell you because I took the bike to the dump. It should have been there." Truthfully, he had smashed the fuel tank and buried it three miles from the house but still on ranch property. It would never be found.

The sheriff added, "The bike was extensively damaged, and I believe it odd I couldn't find the fuel tank."

"The bike was too heavy for me to load, so I used the tractor with its front end loader attachment to load it into my pickup, so by the time it was loaded, I'll admit it was pretty much crunched. I still don't know why you couldn't find the gas tank."

The sheriff asked if he could visit the ranch and look around.

Carl said "Sure, by all means. Be sure to let me know what day and time you plan your visit so I can have the gate open for you."

The sheriff nodded, knowing full well he'd never find a

thing because everything would be taken care of long before he reached the scene.

THAT NIGHT CARL dreamt he was back aboard the boat with Chi Lou Mei. After they left Vietnam, they skirted Cambodia and reached Thailand. Working daily with her and not knowing any Chinese was a real challenge, but they came to the realization they were stuck with each other.

Chi Lou Mei used the sail rather than the engine. She often used the engine in open waters, but when approaching or leaving a port, she was always under sail. It took him a long time to realize she did this to avoid attracting any attention or suspicion. She felt the authorities would become suspicious if she used the engine to travel faster since that would indicate she might be a smuggler and doing something illegal. This didn't set well with him because sailing was so slow. It would take forever to get to Singapore.

Then one night, they were smuggling arms to a freighter when the harbor patrol stopped them. Carl knew this was the end of the line for both of them and prison was their next stop. When the authorities boarded the boat, all they found was tons of produce and jewelry.

What they didn't know was the arms were buried under the produce. There was a false bottom temporarily installed under the produce and the firearms were under the false bottom. Two of the three officers were satisfied with their search of her boat but the fourth officer stayed and continued the search. He removed some of the produce in case they were hiding something under it. He used a probe and poked it down through the produce but when contacting the false bottom, thought he was contacting the true bottom of the boat. Chi Lou Mei conveniently left some jewelry she had on hand to sell in sight while he searched. Carl detected he was demanding information or making accusations and Chi Lou Mei's was repeatedly denying whatever it was he was insisting on. He finally left the boat and Carl watched Chi Lou Mei carefully picking up the jewelry. Carl noticed a few of the exquisite expensive necklaces were missing. It took him a while to understand they weren't really stolen, it was a method Chi Lou Mei used to bribe the man. He could take the bribe without verbalizing the fact or facing her. When the arms were delivered to the freighter, Chi Lou Mei got in an argument with them about the produce. They didn't want it, and its poor quality wasn't the only issue. They didn't need any. She made such a fuss they finally took it. The freighter left port before sunrise and Chi Lou Mei was taking her boat out of the harbor shortly thereafter.

Carl awoke once more drenched in sweat, heart pounding, believing he was on his way to prison. He got dressed, fixed coffee, and spent the rest of the night on the porch. *Damn the dreams. If I'm not back in the prison, I'm killing one of those soldiers, running for my life through the jungle, or back with Chi Lou Mei.*

16

THE WILL

Connie walked into the house with the mail and noticed a letter from attorneys, Alexander and Willis, and wondered what this was about. "Did you know your mother had a will?" she asked Fred in an unbelieving tone after reading the letter.

"No, why?"

"This letter is informing us of a date for the reading of Carol's will. They want us in their office at 2:00 PM on Wednesday, two weeks from now."

"When in the hell did this come about? I never dreamed mom had a will. Oh well, it's probably only a formality. I wonder if it will clear up the problem of Carl and the north half. I'll bet we're going to find out the truth about the crap Carl has pulled and we'll be able to get the law to evict him. It'll be great to see the last of him and his crap."

While eating dinner, Fred shook his head and remarked once more, "I still can't believe mom had a will."

"Does that mean you guys have to go to some law office for a will reading, sort of like on those TV shows?" Inquired Bill?

"Yes, it's two Wednesdays from now at 2:00 PM. I sure hate to have to give up part of the day for it but it might solve the issue with your uncle Carl. There's nothing better I'd like to do than have the sheriff run Carl off the north range. He thinks he's pulled a real fast one on us but I'll show him."

THREE DAYS later Mike saw Sharon at school and while chatting, mentioned the will. Dad was really unhappy about having to take time away from his chores."

"When will this happen?" Sharon asked.

"Two weeks from now but I don't remember what time. It's in the afternoon, that's all I remember. I think Uncle Carl will have to move after that." Mike replied.

While eating dinner Sharon commented, "Mom, can Carl be chased off of his farm?"

"Why do you ask, honey?"

"Mike told me something about a will being read and then sending Carl away."

"Did Mike tell you when this was going to take place?"

"Yes, in two weeks, the same day I have dance lessons."

"That would be Wednesday; did he tell you what time?"

"I don't remember. He might have."

The next day after work Donna drove out to the ranch to see Carl and tell him of the reading of the will.

"Did you get a letter about it?"

"No but they might not know where to send it. That or I'm not invited."

"Can they take the ranch away from you?"

"I don't know, I have the title to the land but if the will reads something else, it could end up in probate and God only knows what would take place then. They could win because they can afford a lawyer whereas I can't."

"What are you going to do?"

"I don't know but I'd sure like to hear what is read."

CARL HAD the day narrowed down but not the time so he drove in and parked far enough down the street so he could see if and when Fred visited the local attorney's office. Carl could only hope it was this office and not one of those in Deer Lodge.

MR. ALEXANDER SHOOK hands with Fred and Connie and had them sit at a conference table and as he sat down, announced, "I'm glad you came in for this formality and I'm sure you understand your mother had specific desires concerning the land.

In any case, allow me to get started."

The door opened, a secretary let the person behind her in. Carl walked in and found a chair.

"What do you think you're doing here; I don't believe any of this is your business so you can leave." demanded Fred.

"Excuse me gentlemen, but are you, Carl Weston?"

"Yes sir." replied Carl.

"Please take a seat and I will continue."

Alexander started reading:

"I, Carol Louise Weston, having sound mind and body desire to have the ranch lands handled as follows, but some history first:

The two brothers Winston and Frederick Weston wanted to purchase and run the ranch. Winston Weston provided 50% of the purchase cost as a down payment and the rest of the loan was to be shared equally and Frederick and I were to pay 50% of the down payment back to Winston, Frederick's brother.

Winston worked on the ranch for 10 years at which time he married and moved to town and got other employment. Six years later Winston Weston and his wife died when their home burned and we took in their son, five year old Carl Weston. Carl continued to live with us until 1962, a total of 12 years. We raised Carl as one of our own.

During this time, Frederick married Connie, and had William and Michael.

It is my desire that due to my husband Frederick and his brother Winston purchasing the ranch and the fact we were never able to pay the portion of the down payment to Winston and his wife due to their deaths, I have bequeathed the southern half of the ranch to my son Fred and the northern half of the ranch to my husband's brother's son Carl.

"Well shit, that's one fine how do you do." Fred yelled as his fist slammed down on the table while getting up to leave.

Still yelling, "I don't believe this. Mom and Dad raised that ungrateful turd and she did this. They paid back every dime they owed Uncle Winston by raising his kid. Can this be contested?"

"You could try but being as how it's a legal will, it would take years and lots of time to sort out. I'm sorry if it wasn't as you expected but you have to understand, your mother held the title due to inheriting it as the wife of your father and it is her last will and testament. Keep in mind, if Carl's parents hadn't been killed in the fire, and let's say your parents had paid back that fifty percent of the down payment, both brothers would still share ownership. I'm sure that is how your mother saw it in her eyes." explained Mr. Alexander.

"My family just got screwed, that's what you're telling me. My wife and three kids got the shaft. We've worked that ranch all our lives and Carl drops in after being gone for darn near 20 years..."

"17 to be exact." interjected Connie.

"I'm sorry, I wasn't aware this was going to be this disturbing for any of you. When your mother, Carol had me write up this will, everything appeared to be extraordinarily equitable." replied Mr. Alexander while thinking, *Carol mentioned there might be some differences of opinion but she certainly didn't indicate this amount of discontent.*

On the drive home, Connie asked, "Did you know about Carl's dad paying fifty percent of the ranch's down payment?"

"No, that was all news to me; I guess Mom and Dad

just never talked about it. I couldn't believe what I was hearing, God that makes me so damn mad. How could Mom do this to us? That turd doesn't deserve any part of this ranch."

Connie didn't say another word on the drive home but thought, "He is you cousin. You may hate him, like he hate's Charlie, the Viet Cong who tortured him in the prison camp, but he is still your blood. I wonder how much Donna knows about Carl and his past?" She shuddered as this crossed her mind.

17

THE SWING SET

Donna and Sharon came to visit mostly because Sharon had been pestering her for several days; she wanted to play in the dirt and make her own garden. Donna wanted to see Carl too but didn't want to be a pest either. She had things to get done at home and so did Carl, but she still gave in to Sharon. When they arrived, Carl invited them into the house. Sharon saw the swings Carl had built for her and wanted to go swing. The three of them went and Carl pushed Sharon.

Donna sat on the other swing and Carl said, "I'll be right back," and went into the house. He wasn't gone long, but he felt he'd never get the courage to do this again, so it was now or never.

As he returned, he stepped behind Sharon, gave her

two more pushes and walked around in front of Donna and asked, "Donna, will you marry me?" Donna wasn't expecting the question, so her mind whirled.

Without thinking, she blurted, "What about Sharon?"

Carl's mind went into overdrive, and he wondered what she was asking. He was expecting a yes or a no answer, not a question. He instantly thought, *I didn't think this through well enough.*

Being this far off guard and out of his element, he blurted, "Well you know the old saying: love me, love my dog."

Donna was still looking at him with big eyes.

That was so dumb. I really muffed this all to hell. Carl added, "Maybe I'm asking you if I can adopt Sharon. Like I said, "I'd like to hold you forever."

Donna stood up and said, "Yes," and kissed him. She reached her hand out and let Carl put the ring on her finger. She saw it wasn't expensive, though it had several small diamonds on it and a small ruby, Sharon's birthstone.

Sharon jumped off the swing and enthusiastically asked. "Is Carl going to be my daddy?"

18

CARL AND DONNA'S WEDDING

1981

Carl knocked on Donna's door the night before their wedding, Sharon opened it with a squeal, "Carl's here."

Carl stepped in as Donna entered the room from the kitchen. "I want you to have this and I'm hoping you will wear it tomorrow." Carl handed the well-worn cloth bag to Donna, *he flashed back to being on the wharf and leaving Chi Lou Mei's boat for the last time. He'd walked a few paces when Chi Lou Mei called him back. He turned around and she approached him with a small bag in her hands. "You take, you keep, very powerful, bring good luck, maybe bribe official, or give to special woman. She had never given him anything except the clothes he needed and the meals she fixed for the three of them.*" This was special so as he took the cloth bag, he gave Chi Lou Mei a deep bow.

Carl's time working on the fish wharf and warehouse was strenuous and tiring. His small one room living quarters were cramped but he didn't need much room because all he had were clothes, toiletries, and the small bag Chi Lou Mei gave him. He decided to look in the bag to see what she had given him. Shocked at what he found, he instantly understood her parting words, "You take, you keep, very powerful, bring you good luck, maybe bribe official or give to special woman." as he removed a beautiful jade necklace from the bag. The necklace comprised of two strands of jade beads, one strand shorter than the other and they were attached in the back. Each strand had a sequence of two small beads and one large bead with each large bead becoming larger as it approached the middle, the lowest point of the necklace. At that lowest point, a large jade dragon formed the focal point of the necklace. He instantly knew she had valued him as a shipmate, something he worked hard to make sure she had to depend on him but he was never sure how she felt. The necklace was expensive in the orient, stateside it was worth a fortune.

Donna gasped as she removed the necklace from the bag. "It's beautiful, where did you get it?"

"Chi Lou Mei gave it to me when I left her boat in

Singapore." She told me, 'you keep, very powerful, bring good luck, maybe bribe official, or give to special woman.' You are the special woman that its good luck brought me."

Donna thanked Carl with a kiss on the cheek then ran him out of the house. She didn't want to break any traditions of not being seen before the wedding.

DONNA WAS GETTING READY, Connie helped her put the Jade necklace on and while helping her put on the pair of green earrings she was loaning Donna for the occasion, commented, "Your necklace is beautiful. I hope you won't mind wearing these green earnings of mine, though, they're not the same shade of green as your necklace."

"They're beautiful Connie, thank you for letting me wear them."

The small wedding was held in the small country church on the outskirts of town. Connie, Donna's matron of honor, gave Fred an excuse to go into town so he wouldn't know where she was going or why. She changed her clothes at Donna's. The auto shop owner was Carl's best man, and Sharon was the flower girl. Four of Donna's work friends attended and the mechanic at the auto shop also attended.

Carl wore the best clothes he had though added a

sports coat and tie. Donna insisted he wear a tie and not his bolo tie.

Once the music started, Carl turned toward Donna coming up the aisle. Carl thought she looked radiant as she walked down the aisle with her brother.

She was wearing a tea length satin dress with a lace overlay, a V neck back and short sleeves. Seeing the jade necklace around her neck made him smile a little bigger. She was also wearing low heeled shoes with silver buckles and in her hands was her bouquet of corn flowers and Montana sand wort.

Their vows were short and sweet, just the way they both wanted them.

Afterwards, Donna's work friends from the school supplied treats and little sandwiches. Donna had made sure there was coffee, punch, and a wedding cake her sister-in-law made.

THE FOLLOWING MONTH, Donna, Carl, and Sharon drove to Dear Lodge for their appointment with the court to finalize Carl's adoption of Sharon. Carl wore the same clothes he wore for their wedding and Donna wore one of her nice dresses she kept for special occasions. Sharon wore a pretty dress and her hair pinned up with barrettes.

They were invited into the judge's chamber and asked what seemed like a thousand questions; though many of them had already been answered in the legal forms they had submitted. The proceeding took forty-five minutes and at the end of the questioning, the judge pronounced to Sharon, "You are now legally, Sharon Weston."

With a big smile on her face, Sharon gave her Mom and new Dad Carl, a big hug.

19

SEVEN YEARS LATER

After being married at thirty-six, the next seven years were full of hard work but at forty-three, Carl was happy with the ranch. It prospered and Carl was able to buy a new four-wheel drive pickup for general use. Granted, working with Fred and Connie had its frustrations, though keeping everything on a business basis enabled both families to learn to at least keep civil and run the ranch.

Carl had also purchased two horses and learned to ride. He spent the time and money on riding lessons because he wanted to use the horses when inspecting the fence lines and portions of the property where it was too rough for the pickup. The far northern portions included rough and mountainous terrain. While riding those areas, he always had fence-mending equipment with him and made sure he was armed. One never knew what critters, two legged, four legged or no legged might be encountered.

Carl also taught both Donna and Sharon how to ride and shoot. The last thing he wanted was for one of them to ride into the backcountry or portions of the property and not be armed. As she got older, Sharon took to riding like a duck to water and enjoyed riding by herself. She often accompanied Carl so he made sure she knew the lay of the land and used to riding in rough country.

DURING ONE OF HIS RIDES, he encountered two people he surmised were hunters, though on a neighbor's fenced land and not his. As he approached, he saw it was two young boys exploring. By the time Carl got within two hundred yards, he could see they were taking turns watching him through binoculars. He ignored them and but new they were watching him, probably trying to discover who he was. Later, word got passed around at school behind Sharon's back that her father looked like a cowboy riding the range in the movies, except he also looked like he was still in Vietnam with his boonie hat.

ONCE WHILE RIDING the fence line, Sharon—being sixteen and still learning to ride--was accompanying Carl. As they approached a small ravine and creek, they discovered a small camp located in a ravine. It would be next to impossible to find unless one approached from the fence line, followed the ravine to avoid detection rather than cresting the hogback, and sky-lining oneself. Carl stayed off the ridge tops so he wouldn't be sky-lined though due to the fence location, he often had to ride a ridge to check the fence. He didn't want uninvited guests such as trespassers on the property, so he gathered all of their equipment, followed their trail to the fence line, and dumped it all on the other side of the fence.

He later placed a "Private Property, No Trespassing" sign on the fence at that location. The neighbor wasn't happy with him dumping the camping equipment on their property, but that's where the trespassers had accessed Carl's land from. As far as Carl was concerned, the trespassers had crossed the neighbor's land to get to his, so he was moving their equipment back along the trail they had used to encroach on his property.

20

DALE

Dale Miller worked on ranches and in real estate, but he always wanted a ranch of his own. The day he found a ranch for sale, he found a realtor in the yellow pages and phoned to ask questions. The ranch wasn't as big as some, but it was affordable for Dale. Granted, he had to drive from Billings to some small town he'd never heard of, an hour's drive from Deer Lodge. As it was, he was able to stay with a cousin in Deer Lodge and commute to see the ranch. The first impression was the place needed fixing up. The main house hadn't been lived in for a year as the ranch had been foreclosed upon. The outbuildings also needed some work, but nothing too drastic.

After visiting the ranch for the first time and before

driving back to Dear Lodge he stopped in at a local café for dinner and discovered he wasn't used to such a friendly and efficient wait staff. The lady who waited on him asked if his day was going well and if she could get him something to drink. Throughout his meal, she came by several times to check to see if he wanted anything and made sure his coffee cup was never empty.

The meal was good and being happy with the service, he decided to eat there on his second time in town. Once more the same lady waited on him and made sure he wanted for nothing. She also wished him a pleasant evening as he left.

Dale didn't know why, but he liked her service and the fact she took time to talk with him a little. After eating there several times, he discovered when her slower time was and made it a point to stop during those hours.

After eating at the cafe on five different occasions, he asked the lady, "So I don't have to call you 'Hey you,' what's your name?"

She replied, "Susan."

Dale surprised himself and he couldn't explain why but he was attracted to her. This was a total foreign feeling because a diner was the last place he'd ever envisioned meeting a woman. The friendly tall waitress with the big smile and beautiful, long, jet black hair drew him to the diner like a magnet.

She wasn't skinny, but she wasn't overweight either. She made an odd expression as he asked her what her name was.

He wasn't sure if she was expecting a complaint or what, but a look of concern certainly crossed her face. He wanted to know her name so he could call her by her name, making his compliments more personal.

Susan had gotten used to his regular dining visits, so she often spent a little more time chatting with him and was intrigued when he informed her; he was purchasing a nearby ranch. At first, she thought he was trying to lead her on, but she ruled that out the minute he described its location to her. She knew exactly what ranch he was trying to buy. His comment about it being next door to the one with the big, tall gate with the wagon wheels and sign reading "Weston Ranch.

He went on to tell her he had to drive south on the highway past a roadside fruit stand and ten miles past the big ranch to get to the one he was putting money down on. The only clothes Susan saw him wear were dress cloths so not being dressed like a rancher, she asked, "Have you worked or run a ranch?"

Dale replied, "I worked on ranches for several years and helped my cousin run his, outside of Deer Lodge.

Dale ate at the café off and on for four weeks. One time while eating his dinner, waited for Susan to come and refill his coffee cup, he asked her, "Would you like to go to a concert in Deer Lodge with me? The band Supertramp will be playing." He knew right away she was shocked at the question and she stood there for several seconds with indecision on her mind. He showed her the two tickets hoping she'd say yes.

It took Susan several moments to get over the surprise because most people didn't treat her nicely. Granted, this fellow was new in town, so maybe he would be different. The scary part was she'd have to go with him to Deer Lodge alone. At first, she didn't answer because she had to mull it over in her mind.

Dale was disappointed and figured he muffed it and scared her off with his offer. At the counter while paying his bill, she took his money and, nodded her head and said, "Yes, I actually like their music. I would love to go with you."

THE NIGHT of the concert Dale picked her up, the first thing Susan noticed was he dressed casually but nice. She had spent several hours worrying about what to wear. This was a date and she wanted to look nice but didn't have a lot of date type clothes to choose from. One didn't dress to the nines for a rock concert so she finally chose a skirt and a complimenting blouse.

After Dale helped her into his car while closing his door, commented, "Wow, you look nice tonight."

She responded with a "Thank you," as she tried to deal with her trust issues and worried about how this evening was going to go. Susan's mind wouldn't let her completely relax since she'd never had good experiences with dates. The two she'd been on didn't go well...

While driving back from the concert, Dale thanked her for her companionship. Susan found it hard to believe he took her straight to the concert. After the concert, took her to an all-night café where he bought them each a desert, and after eating drove her straight home. Not once did he try to enter her space or put his hands on her. As he walked her to her door, he asked, "May I see you again sometime?"

"I had a real good time this evening, and yes, I believe I would like that."

The following weeks Dale didn't eat at the café quite so often, but after a few weeks, he again asked Susan if she'd like to go out with him. "It'll be just a cruise if you will. I'll show you my new ranch."

"You bought it?" Susan excitedly replied.

"Yes, but now I have lots of work to do to get it in operating condition and last but not least, profitable."

"I'd love to go see it."

THE FOLLOWING week he took her to see the ranch and walked her through the house and barns. She saw it would take a lot of work. As he explained it, the structures were sound, so he'd be able to do most of the work himself. In her eyes, he didn't look like the carpenter type, but who was she to judge?

During the next six months, Susan didn't see much of Dale except for once a week when he came to town for supplies. He always made it a point to stop in to see Susan, though in her mind, he was there to eat and no other reason. She didn't know the real reason and Dale didn't help the situation because all he talked about was fixing stuff at his ranch.

Once more he surprised her by asking her if she'd like to see everything he'd done on the ranch. She accepted and enjoyed her trip to his ranch. Once more, he was genuinely nice to her and while going through the house, kept asking her, "What would you do with this room? What color would you paint this room?" On and on, she didn't understand why he didn't paint it the way he wanted it; why ask her?

During one of these outings, Dale included a drive

north farther into the mountains and stopped at a viewpoint. The view of the countryside was nice, but it was the sunset he wanted to enjoy with her. As the sun went down, he could feel the air getting colder. It was this moment Dale took to step closer to her and put his arms around her and pulled her against him. Susan wasn't used to people getting too close, but his warmth made her feel good inside. She didn't move so she could savor the moment.

Over the next few months, Dale would take Susan to the ranch and she helped him paint all the rooms. He had her choose all the colors and asked her opinion on how he should remodel the kitchen. At first, he always had a picnic lunch made for them, but after several weekend workdays, she started bringing enough for a complete evening meal; that way they didn't have to go to the café to eat.

It took several months to get the house remodeled, floors sanded and finished, new kitchen, and the rooms painted. During this time Dale purchased livestock so he could try and get the place to pay for itself. Dale chose a nice fall day to bring Susan to the ranch, after walking her through the house, he took her into the back yard where they could sit and enjoy one of the last warm fall days.

"Do you like the house? Dale asked.

"Yes, of course I like it. I see that you made all the changes I suggested."

Once more, a trust issue and depressing worry entered her mind, "After all the work she helped him with, was he going to dump her and stop seeing her? She enjoyed his company, working on the house with him, and liked being with him. But was all this just a way to get free work? Darn, she was such a pushover. She hoped he liked her better than that.

After the way others treated her in grade school and high school, she had a natural defense of not trusting others so it was hard to get close to him now, all the time wondering when he would do something to hurt her. Granted, throughout the year, he had held her hand on many occasions and at times hugged her. The last several times while working in the house and helping him put personal items in closets and cupboards, he had kissed her. She liked the feel of his arms around her but still found kissing hard. Too many people had made fun of her throughout the years, so she was self-conscious and often asked herself, 'What does Dale see in me. Is he being honest and genuine while being nice to me? Does he like me?' She couldn't question him too closely because there were many things she never discussed and the things that took place in school were something she never wanted him to know.

It was this one last nice fall afternoon while having lunch under the big tree, Dale was telling her of his next plans for the ranch.

They had finished eating and he pulled out a bottle of wine. As he poured wine into two glasses he commented, "I want to celebrate our accomplishments, and I have one more thing to ask. Will you marry me?"

Susan didn't expect that question, and in shock, covered her mouth with both hands. *Oh, oh, she's not ready for this* was Dales first thought.

After a moment, Susan uncovered her mouth and said, "Yes."

Before Dale could react, she was hugging him tighter than he'd been hugged by anybody and he could tell she was crying.

Susan was so happy she couldn't stop her tears. This friend wanted her and she loved him too.

Dale wasn't sure what to think as he could feel Susan's tears on his neck and shoulder, but she was holding him so darn tight, it was something she never did so it surprised him.

Later after some wine and more hugs, they walked hand-in-hand to the house and inside. Susan was once more emotional knowing he had let her choose the colors of her house, do most of the remodeling, and it would be her home. She'd love him till the end of time. She never dreamed she'd be married at forty-four, believing all along no one would ever want her. They got married in the spring of the following year.

A YEAR after they were married, Dale was in the hardware store and one of the other customers asked him if he'd met his neighbor. "No, why?" he replied.

"Carl Weston—the Vietnam veteran living on the northern portion of the Weston ranch swindled half of the ranch from his cousin Fred Weston. The guy's half nuts and rides his fence line like an armed guard."

Dale didn't exactly like Fred Weston, but since Dale never did business with him, he didn't know him. Dale didn't care who was next door as long as they didn't encroach on his land. Susan never wanted to get closer to any of their neighbors, so as far as he was concerned, if Susan wasn't interested, he wasn't interested. None of them approached him or appeared to open any kind of friendship, so he left it at that. He was also aware of Susan's lack of befriending other people much less their neighbors. She still worked at the café and he knew she was their best waitress.

When he returned home, he mentioned what he heard in town and Susan commented, “Don’t believe everything you hear.” Dale thought about what she said, was she defending Carl or warning him to disregard rumors.

21

SUSAN

Carl was riding the fence line and the summer day was warmer than usual. Looking to the west he saw a large thunderhead and knew a bad storm was moving in. Being miles from home, he decided to avoid the storm by visiting his neighbor's ranch rather than trying to get home in a driving rainstorm. As he rode into the neighbor's yard, it was getting late. Before he dismounted, the neighbor came out and asked, "Are you lost?" Carl explained his situation. He introduced himself to the landowner; he knew this neighbor was new to the area. Well, new as of sometime in the last fifteen years. In any case, he would be happy if he would be able to stay dry and out of the storm.

Carl asked if he could put his horse in the barn. He added he would be happy being allowed to sleep with the horse. Carl also told the neighbor he was a non-smoker so he didn't have to worry about fire. Carl discovered he didn't know this neighbor, Mr. Miller.

As Dale walked back into the house, Susan asked, "Who was the rider and what did he want?"

"It was Carl, the fellow from next door. I don't trust him, and from what I've heard in town, I don't want him around. You know, most people come up here in a vehicle rather than on horseback, looking like they left a war zone. He wanted to stay the night in the barn with his horse and will leave as soon as the weather clears, hopefully by morning."

Susan replied, "We have an extra room and bed. You could have invited him in rather than having him sleep in the barn."

Dale replied, "From what I've heard, he somehow took control of half of the ranch from the legal owner, Fred Weston. No, I don't want him around; he can sleep in the barn."

Susan couldn't help feeling bad because of Dale's rude treatment of a neighbor, and all through dinner and while cleaning up, she felt guiltier, and guiltier. Eventually, she couldn't help herself; she had to go and at least talk to him.

The name Carl Weston brought back the memory of the worst day of her life. She wasn't pretty and when in school, her classmates had teased and made fun of her. She wasn't popular and she was only dated twice in high school. Both boys took her to a movie and after the movie; all they wanted to do was make out and test her boundaries. It hurt knowing they only took her out to see how far they could go.

There was that awful day in high school, Deric Hollingsworth had grabbed her purse and ran around the classroom with it. She chased him and tried to catch him, but looking back, she realized he would never have allowed her to catch up. He played with her by letting her almost catch up and then sprinted to the front of the class and dumped everything in her purse onto the floor. It was so humiliating to hear her classmates laughing and chanting "Go Deric, go Deric." She'd never been so humiliated or shamed in her life than that moment when her spare pair of panties and other feminine items got dumped on the floor in front of the class, with both boys and girls in attendance.

She could still hear Deric's scream and see his blood splatter on the wall as Carl's fist hit his face when she recalled that day. She was so angry with her classmates for their chants and the approval they gave Deric. To add her anger, Carl had acted as if nothing happened and walked to the front of the class and started picking up some of her belongings. The thought of him or anybody touching her stuff infuriated her. It was her stuff, and when he started picking her stuff up, the class started chanting, "Carl love's Susan." She always wished she had never gone to school that day. It was the last time she saw Carl because the teacher came in and sent him to the office and he was expelled from the school.

They weren't friends, and she couldn't recall Carl ever speaking to her, but he was the only person in the school who didn't put up with other people's mistreatment. He never took a wooden nickel from anybody. It was three years later when the realization hit her one night, she actually cried knowing he was expelled from school for helping her. None of her other classmates ever bothered to help or befriend her. She absolutely never talked about that day. That was a day she never wanted people to remember. She still felt shame and guilt every time she remembered it.

She didn't have enough money to attend college, so she got a job at the café in town. She liked working there because she got to hear and keep up with the latest news, gossip, and goings-on in town. The pay wasn't bad, and she did well with tips from the local ranchers when and if they came into town.

It was at the café where she met her husband, Dale. He was new in town and didn't know how she had been treated in school.

Dale loved her, treated her nice and they got along well. He made her happy because he treated her well, and while dating, he never tried to take advantage of her. He was the one person who appreciated her loyalty and love. One day he confided, he liked the fact she never talked badly about others. Well, she tried to never live in the past, and once married, she was able to leave school days behind, though she knew a couple of female classmates who still avoided her when they ate at the café. The few times Deric came in, she found it hard to wait on his table much less smile. He never left a tip either unless his wife was with him.

After Susan put the dinner dishes away, she put on her jacket and walked out to the barn. Knowing Carl was there was like a magnet, drawing her forward, like a moth to a flame. Not because she liked him, but because she was sad for what took place those years ago and wondered what had taken place since she heard he was MIA.

As Susan approached the person lying on some hay bales that had been lined up for a bed, she said, "Hello." All she heard in reply was a grunt, had she made a big mistake coming to the barn, "Carl?" she asked.

The figure covered with a blanket uncovered his head and said, "Yeah?"

She apologized for disturbing him and added her apologies for her husband putting him in the barn.

Carl said, "It's fine, don't worry about it."

Susan, sensing how awkward this was, asked how he got caught in the storm. Carl sat up and explained he was riding the fence line, which he tried to do three or four times a year, and the freak storm caught him. By this time she noticed his saddle nearby and the rifle in the saddle scabbard hanging from it. At the same time, she could see his face and voice; it certainly wasn't the Carl she remembered.

She asked him, "What happened to you?" Carl gave her an abbreviated rendition of what took place in Vietnam.

Suddenly she had the urge to change the subject before that awful day in class came up. She commented, "You married the school secretary, Donna, didn't you?"

Carl replied, "Yes, and meeting Donna is one of the best things that's ever happened to me."

Susan could relate to that comment, she felt the same about the day she met Dale.

By this time Dale realized she wasn't in the house and went to the barn, he was surprised to see Carl sitting on one of the hay bales and Susan seated on a bucket she had turned upside down. He was surprised Susan had come out to talk to this fellow he'd heard nothing good about.

What possessed his wife to come and talk to him. Dale's first impression made him think Carl was one of those survivalist types. Dale had absolutely no use for them and looking closer saw the only camo Carl had was his boonie hat. Most survivalists tended to wear more camo than what Carl was wearing. The clothes didn't fit the description and neither did his rifle. Rather than a semi-automatic firearm, Carl's bolt action rifle looked like some relic dating back to the turn of the century, maybe WWI.

Dale gave Susan an excuse to return to the house but as she left, she informed Carl breakfast would be on the table at 6:00 AM.

Carl didn't make breakfast as he was long gone, since he woke at 4:00 AM and the rain had stopped.

22

SHARON

Sharon's high school years were filled with helping her mother harvest the vegetables they grew in their garden and selling them at a roadside stand they had beside the highway where the ranches' gravel drive met the state highway. Sharon liked to go horseback riding when the weather was nice too. On many occasions, she went riding with Carl. She was becoming a nice-looking young lady and was getting good grades in school.

While in high school, the topic of school dances came up. Carl told her she could go but wanted her home at a reasonable hour afterwards. He also explained, "The longest walk a boy can make is walking across the dance floor to ask a girl to dance. In a young boy's mind, everyone is looking at him and when he gets turned down, he feels like a cur dog slinking off with its tail tucked between its legs. So here's a ground rule: any time a boy asks you to dance, you are to accept the request and you are to dance with each boy at least one time. Granted, you might not want to dance with every classmate you have, but I want you to at least dance one dance with each boy who asks. I don't care if he's tall, short, black, white, native, or ugly; you accept the offer at least one time."

The day finally arrived when she was asked out, and a young lad, Thomas, arrived to pick her up. It was awkward because Thomas had to have his mother do the driving. When he came to the door and Sharon let him in and introduced him to her mother and father. Thomas got tongue-tied and didn't know what to say. Faced with Sharon's father, a man with a scarred face and a low rasping voice, his brain reran all the stories he heard about her father at school. The sooner he could get out the door the better, but Sharon was telling him she'd be a couple more minutes.

Oh boy, he didn't want to have to answer any of her father's questions. In Thomas' mind, it was pure hell having to tell Sharon's mom and dad his mother was driving them.

Carl knew exactly how Thomas felt but he wasn't going to make it easy for him. To kill time while Sharon was getting ready, he asked Thomas how school was going for him. Thomas couldn't help but see the 1911 .45 Colt ACP on the table being field stripped and cleaned. Carl had been wearing it for several days while riding fence lines, so it needed to be wiped down and oiled.

Sharon entered the room looking beautiful, said goodbye to her parents, and they left for the dance.

The following Monday, Thomas' friends asked him how his date had gone, he told them about Sharon's father. He didn't mention how horribly uncomfortable he was while waiting for Sharon. He liked Sharon, but never asked her for another date.

The following year another young lad named Bill asked her to the prom. The evening he arrived to get Sharon, Carl saw the Camaro he was driving. Carl had his Enfield 1917 30-06 leaning against the wall beside his chair. Like Thomas, Bill had to wait a few minutes for Sharon and while waiting, Carl asked him, "How fast does your car go?"

Bill, being used to talking to other kids, or adults at the auto shop replied, "I've had it up to 100 MPH."

Carl responded with, "You go that fast with my Sharon and I'll break your damn neck."

Donna asked him what time he would be bringing Sharon home.

He didn't have an answer. "You'll have her home no later than 12:00 PM." Carl interjected. This gave him time to treat her to something after the dance and still have time to drive her home. It didn't allow much time, but it was done on purpose.

Sharon entered the room looking stunning in her light blue dress. As they were walking out the door, Bill noticed the rifle, an M1 Garand, hanging above the front door. He didn't say a word to Sharon till they were in the car. He didn't know what to say after dealing with her father.—his scarred face and low growling voice made those moments in her house quite uncomfortable.

Bill got her home by 12:00 PM, and Sharon reminded him to be sure to close the gate after he drove through. The next morning she got up early enough to ride her horse to check on the gate. Bill had left it open, which angered Sharon because gates should never be left open unless one finds them open. Bill had committed a grave error, and she never dated him again.

On ranches, it's a cardinal sin to leave a closed gate open after you've gone through it.

During Sharon's last school year, Carl's cousin Mike took her to a couple of movies and during the summer, to the rancher's co-op picnic.

Sharon had an interesting surprise the day Mike took her to the county fair. Mike treated her like a sister all day but later in the evening on the Ferris wheel, Mike put his arm around her and held her much closer than usual.

Sharon didn't mention it to her mother and father but she had enjoyed the day and evening with him.

The following month, he took her to the rodeo and to the dance afterwards. He was able to have her home by 11:00 PM and since he had a key, locked the gate on his way home. Sharon enjoyed being with Mike but she wasn't sure how to react to his getting too close because being adopted by Carl, she was Mike's cousin. He was always good to her and she enjoyed being with him but being adopted by Carl added to her confusion. Her biological father wasn't part of the family, she wasn't a blood relative, but the family situation sure made their relationship awkward to say the least. It certainly wasn't something she felt she could discuss with her mother or father.

Upon graduating from high school, Sharon applied for jobs but didn't get any replies. While waiting for job opportunities, she helped her mother with the vegetable garden, prepared the produce, and helped sell them at their roadside stand.

One thing Carl insisted on, when manning the roadside stand, both Donna and Sharon had to be present. At no time was either of them to be alone at the stand.

23

MIKE

1990

Several months after the county fair, Connie stopped by to visit with Donna. Fred's health wasn't the best; he had high blood pressure and was finding it hard to get around. Connie had to do more and more work at the ranch. JoAnn and her husband were living in Deer Lodge and not interested in the ranch. Bill was in college and not available to help. Mike was trying to help but didn't know what to do or how to do it.

Mike and Sharon spent Sunday in town and while returning to the ranch, had to stop to open the gate. Before Sharon got out, Mike put his arm around her and announced, "I have something for you." as he handed her a small box. She opened it and found a silver necklace. "Thank you, it's beautiful." She explained.

SEVERAL WEEKS LATER, Mike stopped in and asked for Sharon. Once she entered the room, he announced he had joined the Army and would be leaving the following Monday.

Donna wished him well and Carl wished him good luck and smooth sailing. He also commented, "Be damned careful what you volunteer for. Those guys can make you think you're volunteering for a cakewalk, but you soon find yourself in a shit storm. The heroes are all dead so you don't need to be a hero."

Mike said goodbye and turned to leave, Carl stood up from his chair and shook Mike's hand and said, "Take care and watch your back." He wanted to follow Mike out to his car but noticed Sharon was going, so he let the two kids have the little time to themselves. Carl watched them while they were saying goodbye and noticed it wasn't the goodbye a brother and sister or cousin would give each other.

Keeping his own council, he said nothing to Donna.

Carl was cleaning the barn when Sharon walked in and said, "Let's take the horses for a ride?"

Carl thought about it a moment, knowing she never asked him to go with her made him wonder why she was asking at this time and replied, "Sure, start saddling them up and I'll finish this stall."

They rode for half an hour in silence and came to an area where they had a nice view of the valley. Sharon and Carl while still mounted were side by side, she spoke, "Dad, Mike gave this to me just before he left for the Army." She handed Carl the little box.

While looking at the necklace, Carl told her, "It's beautiful."

"I think Mike likes me more than he should and I'm not sure how I should feel.

You're my father so most people think we're cousins. I don't want to hurt anybody, especially you or Mom but since you're not my biological father, Mike and I really aren't related. Is this right or am I missing something?"

"You understand the situation correctly and I understand your quandary. How do you feel about Mike?" Carl asked as he saw Sharon blush and turn her head to face the valley view.

"Have you talked to you mother about this?"

"Yes, she told me to talk to you."

"I appreciate your asking me and I'm not going to be of much help because it's going to be between you and Mike. One thing I will add though, don't worry about what other people think, it's none of their business," advised Carl.

"How close are you and Mike?"

"I don't know, I'm not sure, I like him though."

Carl reached over and lightly squeezed Sharon's arm and said, "Your mother and I will stand behind you no matter what you decide." The mood was much lighter on the return ride back to the barn and Sharon chattered on about how successful the year's harvest was and how much money the produce stand was making.

THE NEXT FOUR years Sharon attended college but returned home each summer to help her mother with the ranch and the produce stand. College was a struggle for her but she managed to keep her grades high enough so she was able to graduate in four years.

Upon returning home, once more she played the job application game with no results. Once more, while waiting for job opportunities, she helped her mother. Donna had a small pickup truck she used for hauling the vegetables and fruit to their stand for sale. Once in a while, Sharon used the truck to run into town, but not often.

24

THE DATE

Jordan Danford and his mother happened to be driving by the produce stand and his mother wanted to stop and buy some of the fresh produce being sold by Sharon and her mother. While his mother was selecting the produce she wanted, Jordan struck up a conversation with Sharon, who was home for the summer from college.

Jordan couldn't help thinking, *she's good looking. I'd like to take her out.* Before they left, he told her he'd see her again soon.

Two days later he stopped by the produce stand and once more chatted with Sharon. During the course of the conversation, he asked, "would you like to go to the movie Friday night? It's the new comedy and it's supposed to be real funny."

"Sure, it sounds like fun." Sharon accepted. She hadn't dated much and didn't have any special understanding with Mike, so at twenty-two years of age, didn't see any reason she shouldn't go on a date to a movie.

Friday evening arrived and Sharon was helping her mother put the unsold produce in the back of their pickup when Jordan arrived. Sharon left with Jordan while her mother drove to the ranch house. Jordan and Sharon had arranged it this way so he wouldn't have to drive the eight miles round trip to the ranch house to pick her up.

After the movie, Jordan told Sharon he wanted to drop by a friend's house. Once inside, Sharon saw, there were lots of people their age in attendance but Sharon didn't know any of them. Jordan grabbed a beer and offered Sharon one, but she said, "No thanks, and I think you'd better take me home now."

Jordan replied, "Right after I finish my beer."

A short time later Sharon discovered people were using drugs in the back room, so she again approached Jordan and asked, "Will you please take me home now?"

Jordan replied, "Okay, give me a couple more minutes." Jordan was hoping Sharon would have a drink or two and loosen up, but it looked like he misjudged her.

A couple minutes later, she was beside him and once more asking him to take her home. Sharon was getting frightened and considered calling her mother. She didn't want to stay at the party one more minute.

Jordan was on his second beer and she again asked, "Please take me home."

Jordan said, "How about if I take you home after we have a couple of dances?"

"No, I want to go home now, I don't want to dance, take me home." She demanded.

Across the room she heard a girl's voice yell, "Jordan, how's it going?"

Jordan responded, "Great. How are you, Janice?"

Sharon figured they knew each other but didn't care. She wanted to leave.

Janice put her arms around Jordan and said, "Let's dance."

They danced two songs before Sharon butted in and said, "Jordan, take me home now."

Jordan looked at Janice and said, "I'll be right back, I have to take our party pooper home."

The comment infuriated Sharon but she didn't say anything. She wanted to leave and get home. After they got in Jordan's car and headed for the ranch, Jordan tried to get back into her good graces and tried to apologize.

Sharon was so darn scared and angry; she didn't say anything in return. Stopping the car at the ranch gate, he leaned over hoping to get a hug and a kiss but Sharon was out of the car before he had a chance and unlocked the gate. Jordan, already angry and Janice was waiting for him, didn't want to drive the three miles to the ranch house and back, so he put the car in reverse, turned around, and left Sharon at the gate.

There weren't many clouds in the sky so the moon lighted the gravel road so Sharon could see the road but she was hurt, angry, and scared. The long walk did her mind good as she slowly calmed down, but she didn't want to face her dad. She was in shock at what that horse's ass did to her. When she walked through the door, her mother being still up asked, "Are you okay? You're later than usual, what happened?"

"I'll tell you in the morning." Sharon answered on her way to her room.

The next morning, being Saturday, her mother was waiting for her. Sharon recounted what had taken place and her mother told her she should have phoned. She or her dad would have gone to get her. Sharon explained she was so frightened she didn't think of it but finally got Jordan to drive her home.

Later that night, Donna related everything to Carl.

On Monday Carl went to the auto shop and used their phone book to look up the Danford name and discovered it was Walter Danford, and the name came rushing back to him. Wouldn't you know, it was one of the football players he had thrashed back in high school. So Jordan was his son.

Carl drove to the address and knocked on the door.

A lady opened the door and said, "Yes?"

Carl introduced himself, and asked if this was the Walter Danford home and was either Walter or Jordan at home?

The lady turned and invited Walter to the door.

Carl explained what Jordan had done to his daughter last Friday night, he took her out for the evening and left her at the ranch gate, one mile off the highway and three miles from her home. She had to walk three miles in the dark to get home. "Please inform Jordan he's not welcome on any of our ranch property and Sharon doesn't want to see him again. Good day." Carl turned and walked back to his pickup.

Walter turned to his wife and said, "I never did like that guy. I never dreamed I see him again, but talk about bad apples; they always seem to turn up at the damnedest times."

His wife asked, "Did Jordan do what that man said he did?"

"You'll have to ask Jordan," was his answer.

Carl awoke in the middle of the night after dreaming of killing those two Viet Cong soldiers. His dreams always had this weird auditory connection for him, making them that much worse. He heard their bones crack while their necks broke in his arms. It was so easy while you had your adrenaline pumping as high as it does while you're in those circumstances. The frightening part of this dream was he saw and felt Walter Danford's neck being broken in his arms.

There wouldn't be any more sleep, so Carl got out of bed, dressed, and walked out onto the porch. After a few minutes, he made coffee so he could sit on the porch and unwind his frazzled nerves. His mind kept repeating the same thoughts, how it all felt so real and so easy, as if it took place yesterday rather than so many years ago.

Seeing Walters face instead of one of the oriental face of a Viet Cong soldier frightened Carl. *What was he capable of doing?*

Later in the morning, Donna came out with a cup of coffee in her hands and asked, "Carl, are you okay?"

"Yeah, I couldn't sleep," giving his standard reply.

The following evening Jordan was playing a video game when his mother came into his room and asked, "What's this I hear about you making some girl walk three miles home?"

"Aw Mom, it was nothing. She kept badgering me, and I was in a hurry to get back to Devin's place. A bunch of friends got together and Janice was there and I wanted to see her. Sharon was pretty mad at me, so I figured she didn't want me to take her all the way to her house."

Jordan's mom said, "We live in a small town, so it doesn't pay to treat people like dirt. That girl is the high school's secretary's daughter, so people are going to find out what you did. I don't ever want to hear of you doing something like that again."

Later in the evening she broached the topic with Walter. His reaction was, "I don't want to talk about it. That guy is bad news. I look at it as if he got a taste of his own medicine."

His wife commented, "I don't care how you feel about that family. Nobody ever treated me like that, and I don't ever want to hear of Jordan doing it again. By the way, was my boss, Roger Wheeling, one of your teammates back in school?"

"Yes, Why?" replied Walter.

"I was handed that girl's job application along with several other applications at the farm supply store the other day. When Mr. Wheeling handed the applications to me, he told me to call the applicants in for an interview in the order of the applications. Sharon's application was at the bottom though she was totally qualified for the job. She was going to be the last one called. Believe me; I lost all of my respect your friend Roger."

"I don't care how you feel, he's a good friend. Her crazy dad destroyed my friend, Pete Holcomb's bike and got away with it."

TWO DAYS later Jordan was visiting his friend Byron Hollingsworth. They were out in the garage, and he commented on meeting the cute girl manning the produce stand out on the highway. "After taking her to a movie, I took her to Devin's party. I was hoping she would have a few drinks and we could make out, but she went Miss Prude on me."

Byron commented, "You're telling me you picked up the Weston girl so you could check out her melons and tomatoes?"

They both laughed at his crude joke.

"What did her dad have to say when you took her home?" Byron asked.

"I didn't. She turned bitchy on me, so when she got out of the car to unlock the gate, I turned the car around and left her there. Her dad stopped by the house the other day and bitched at my dad about it. He said she had to walk three miles to get to the house, but so what, she didn't have to be such a prude."

Byron commented, "If it's the girl I think it is, she and Mike are pretty thick, and I'd say you're walking in quicksand. Was her name Sharon?"

Jordan answered, "Why, Who's this Mike?"

Byron continued, "I think he's her cousin. He's in the army now, but I used to see them in town together, and they're close, closer than most cousins. It wouldn't surprise me if their kissing cousins." They both laughed with a smirk. Byron added, "If you don't believe me, I saw them at the county fair before he got deployed and they were holding hands."

"I guess I've never seen the guy." Jordan's answered.

Byron told him, "He was a couple years behind us in school, and his name is Mike Weston. I think he's in Afghanistan now."

Jordon replied, "If he's in Afghanistan, she's fair game."

Byron's father, Deric Hollingsworth, who was working on his wife's car, interjected, "If you're talking about the girl who runs the produce stand six miles east of town, she's the high school's secretary's daughter. Her mother's married to Carl Weston, the Vietnam veteran jerk who robbed his brother or cousin or whatever of half his ranch. I'd steer clear of that bunch; I've never liked any of them. It wouldn't surprise me if part of his mind is still in Vietnam. I wouldn't trust him any farther than I could spit. He got messed up over there. He still wears combat boots and a boonie hat."

Deric never told or admitted to any of his family members it was Carl who broke his arm and nose. To this day, he couldn't believe what took place, he was having some fun teasing that girl. Hell, back in those days, everybody teased her. Besides, none of the girls in the class liked her.

25

HOWARD

Spring

The spring came in with fury and brought with it many rainstorms, and one storm lasted a week. A number of the ranchers had trouble with pastures being exceedingly soggy, but the Weston ranch wasn't affected since they didn't have any large creeks on their lands.

Carl was in town with Donna and overheard two people talking about the Miller ranch and the fact they had lost most of their winter feed with the loss of the structure it was stored in. Later in the evening, Carl informed Donna of the situation and said he was going to go see if they needed any help.

The next day Carl drove to the Miller ranch, and as he

pulled in and parked, Dale was standing beside another person near the wreckage of the storage shed. As he approached the two, Dale didn't look happy to see him but introduced him to Susan's brother, Howard.

Dale explained what took place; the creek rose higher than it had ever been and destroyed the winter feed shed. Dale said, "Howard's going to help me rebuild the shed, but I'm not sure what to do about the lost feed."

Carl looked around and commented, "Maybe you ought to put the shed in a better location so this can't happen again."

Dale replied, "That's what Howard suggested."

Carl made no bones about it and asked, "Would you like some extra help?"

Howard sighed and answered with, "I'll take all the help I can get."

After some discussion, Carl said he'd bring the tractor with him the next day and go into town with Howard to get lumber and supplies.

That evening after Carl left and while they were eating dinner, Dale couldn't help but ask, "I can't help wondering why Carl came over."

Howard commented, "He's offered to help, and I'll take all the help I can get. This isn't going to be a slap-together a shed type of chore, you know."

Dale was skeptical but decided to keep his own council.

THE NEXT DAY Carl arrived at 8:00 AM and with Howard's help, salvaged what lumber they could. Once the debris of the structure was cleared away, they drove into town to get lumber and building supplies. On the drive into town, Howard asked Carl a couple of questions, and by the time they reached town they were sharing some of the experiences they had while serving in Vietnam. Howard had been in a Seabee battalion and spent many hours in the field repairing heavy equipment and tanks to get them back into running order.

After purchasing supplies and driving back to the ranch, they continued to share service notes--or reminiscing, as some might put it.

After the day's work, Susan asked him to stay for dinner. All the discussion during dinner was concerning where to build the new shed and what to do with the creek.

Dale was uncomfortable having Carl on the property and confided in Susan while getting ready for bed. "Susan, you know I don't trust that guy. Why is he helping us?

Your brother seems to like him but what does he want, people don't do this for nothing."

Susan replied, "I don't know, but Howard's sure happy to have his help. Howard said he wouldn't have time to get all the work done before he had to go back home to work, but with Carl's help, he thinks they can get everything finished."

It took a week to build a pole shed for the winter feed, so they spent the weekend building a small levee along the creek bank. Howard rented a small dozer and front-end loader for moving earth and rocks they placed several feet away from the creek.

Carl planted pasture grass and willow shoots along the four-foot-high levee so the roots would eventually take hold and strengthen the levee against erosion.

That evening Susan asked her brother how the work was going and what was it like working with Carl.

Howard said, "Carl's great help, why?"

Susan replied, "Dale's been concerned about Carl and well, you know, he's not the most communicative person." Susan didn't want to use the words "mentally disturbed" because if she did, her brother would believe Dale thought the same of him, being a Vietnam veteran also.

Howard looked at his sister and said, "Susan, if you had his voice, you wouldn't be as talkative as you are, and that goes for Dale too. By the way, how many of your other neighbors came to help?"

Susan responded, "They probably wish we'd go under so they could buy us out. Remember, Dale paid the full asking price while they were waiting for the price to be reduced. I don't know why Carl came over but I'm glad he did."

"It's a good thing he did otherwise I couldn't have finished everything we had to do."

Howard continued, "Keep in mind; you folks never crapped on him. From what he's told me, there aren't many people here who would give him the time of day and some think he's a nutcase. His words of course. I spent my time in Vietnam and have experienced some of the same old biased opinions." Howard added, "Dale will have to get over it, because without Carl's help, I wouldn't be able to finish the work for you. If I recall, you weren't the most popular person in school, and neither was Carl."

In Howard's mind, this was the understatement of the year.

"You and I both know most of those same people still live in the area and haven't outgrown their childhood animosities. They're the ones who haven't grown up. I dodged all this by moving away. I married a girl from another town. Just like you, Dale was from another area and didn't know you the same as these people. He's a great guy and works hard for the two of you. I'm happy for you, Sis, that it worked out this way. I'll bet you still run into some of those old classmates at the café."

Susan replied, "Yes, and there are a couple of old classmates who avoid me at the café or won't leave a tip."

Howard added, "Well, if they feel that way towards you, add being a Vietnam vet to the mix and guess how they feel about Carl. I'd hate to have walked in Carl's shoes. Being a POW tells me everything. He's been through stuff nobody in this town could ever dream of, much less survive. Yet, survive he did and also made it back home. You and I both know exactly why he hides out on the ranch. I'm surprised you even work at the café and put up with some of these people."

Susan replied, "Most of the customers are friendly and nice, there's only a couple who can't seem to let go of the past. They still live their high school days. They still support the school's sports as if it was yesterday."

Howard added, "Well, like I said, some of us grew up, some of us went to war, and some never grew up. There's a big difference. You know, Sis, there's a federal push to hire veterans. Well, one of the reasons is because so many people have the wrong opinion and think we're all basket cases and can't do a job or get along. Well that's the farthest from the truth; all veteran's need is a chance. Look at me, a heavy equipment operator with plenty of years' experience and vested in the union. I'm able to provide for my family and still have time to take them on vacations. The thing is: I didn't stay here and darn few people know I was in 'Nam. Oh, and by the way, Carl mentioned he's fifty-one, and he's hoping his leg won't bother him as much next year. I think everyone is hoping next year will be a better year."

IN CARL'S DREAM, it was his and Chi Lou Mei's last night in Cambodia. They just cast off the mooring lines in preparation to leave, a man boarded the boat and a heated argument took place between Chi Lou Mei and the man. Eventually she allowed him to sail with them and she charged him a small fortune. Carl was shocked at the price she charged until asking himself, *Why didn't the man cross the Cambodian border –into Thailand on land*? It was obvious the man couldn't cross it legally so needed to be smuggled in.

The next day at sea, the man discovered the illegal firearms stowed under the deck and made a loud and heated argument with Chi Lou Mei. During the argument, he removed one of the firearms and managed to throw it overboard. Fear in Carl's gut went off like a skyrocket, *What was going to happen? Nothing on this trip was legal.*

The argument finally subsided and the man calmed down but it was obvious neither he nor Chi Lou Mei was happy. During the night Carl was aware of a scuffle and a splash beside the boat. The next morning he discovered, the man was no longer onboard and saw blood stains on the deck. The hair on the back of his neck raised as fear ran through his veins and he realized what his shipmate was capable of. He acted as if nothing had taken place and never questioned Chi Lou Mei about it, come what may, whether he liked it or not, he was in this with Chi Lou Mei.

The moment Carl woke, he was drenched in sweat. He went to the kitchen, made coffee, and found his favorite spot on the porch. While sitting on the porch with his coffee, he recalled another predicament they were in.

Smuggling human cargo across an international border could have put the two of them in prison for life. Damn, Chi Lou Mei would do anything when backed into a corner. Two days later, they had her boat on the beach like the sailing ships of old and careened it so they could do the planking repairs it needed.

THE NIGHT after Howard left to return home, Susan was in bed and almost asleep, her mind dragged up something she'd long since forgotten. While lying there, she recalled all of her classmates playing on the merry-go-round at recess one day. They were probably in second grade. As the recess bell rang, the kids pushed Carl off the merry-go-round and ran to the school. Carl picked himself off the ground and brushed the dirt off, he walked over to where she was sitting on one of the swings and pulled her hair real hard and made her cry. Susan was surprised she recalled the incident since it was so long ago. She wondered if Carl remembered pulling her hair and making her cry.

As Susan's mind continued to churn, she remembered Carl had never teased her or picked on her after that incident. It was all the other kids, especially the girls, who wouldn't play with her. Most of her classmates teased her.

She wore the wrong clothes (her mother made most of her clothes, so her dresses and skirts were always longer than the other girls'), the wrong hair style, no makeup, everything; she was never accepted or invited to other girls' parties, much less their homes to play.

While in high school, the teasing and abuse didn't stop, and part of it was the fact she always wore very modest clothes. Her tops never showed any cleavage like the other girls. She hated school because of the teasing. While in grade school, Susan often had her brother play Hopscotch with her. Later in middle school and high school, they played volleyball and badminton together.

Some of the other instances entered her mind.

She sat beside Kathy Dollinger during history class and she still remembered the note Kathy passed to her. *If you want a boyfriend, I will talk to Deric, and if you go out with him and let him show you how to be nice and have fun, you'll have a boyfriend. Yes or No?*

She was appalled.

Why would she ever want to go out with that jerk? If she did what Kathy was implying, Deric would tell his friends and she'd be the laughingstock of the school.

Two days later Kathy sent her another note, *If you don't want to go out with Deric, I can set you up with Carl. He's like you, nobody likes him either. Yes or No?*

It was all she could do to retain her tears so she walked out of class. The tears rolled down her face as she slowly walked home.

As it was, the day Carl broke Deric's arm and nose was the only time anyone did something for her. Well, she couldn't help but wonder if Carl remembered pulling her hair. She also recalled, she entered the classroom crying but the teacher was in a hurry to get class started and paid no attention to her tattling on Carl.

One more long forgotten incident was recalled.

She was walking to her third period class after leaving

her English literature class where they were reading King Arthur, Deric walked up from behind her and bumped his shoulder against her and said, "Hey Mace-Face, you know why your knight in shining armor beat you with his battle mace? Because you're so ugly he thought you were the dragon." He walked away laughing.

Susan had plain features, but was she ugly? The teasing hurt.

Trying to get some sleep, she moved on to happier thoughts.

It was so nice of Carl to help Howard. Maybe we should invite Carl, Donna, and their daughter over for dinner sometime? I'll suggest it to Dale and see what he thinks. I'll present it to him as a thank-you dinner for Carl's help, but who knows; maybe Donna would become a friend. None of our other neighbors associate with us.

A week after receiving the invitation, Carl and Donna went over to the Millers for dinner. Sharon didn't attend because she was working late on the books and wanted everything finished. Carl was quiet during dinner, though halfway through the meal, complimented Susan on the dinner. Being ham, scalloped potatoes, and a tossed green salad, it wasn't elaborate but most certainly wholesome and delicious. Dale wanted to ask Carl so many questions but didn't want to ruin Susan's evening so found it awkward trying to invite small talk. Carl with his low gravelly voice wasn't into small talk and didn't invite questions.

Susan and Donna hit it off once Susan commented, "Without your produce stand, I don't know what I'd do."

Dale added, "Is that where you get our vegetables and melons?"

"Yes," replied Susan, "I like their produce because it's fresh."

After that comment, Donna and Susan chatted nonstop about vegetables, squash, melons, gardening, and ways to preserve food.

After dinner, Susan asked if anyone would like coffee. Carl answered, "I'll take some, thank you."

After Susan fixed coffee and the others had cold lemonade, they retired to the front porch where it was cooler. Carl was afraid bygone days might come up, and he didn't want to discuss any part of them. He was incredibly happy Susan never mentioned school days. He recalled how the girls treated Susan and presumed she buried those memories because none of them were good.

Susan chatted with Donna but made sure Dale stayed on ranching and equipment problems. Dale found it difficult because Carl didn't say much, didn't feel comfortable trying to make conversation. Dale refilled their cups and suggested they leave the ladies and visit the barn. After entering the barn, they talked cattle and ranching for a while.

Dale commented, "Susan said the two of you were classmates in school."

"Affirmative on that, and you ended up with the nicest girl of the class too."

"Were you and Susan friends in school?"

Carl wondered if Dale was a jealous husband and answered honestly, "No, we had different circles of friends. She lived in town and I was on the ranch. Most of us ranch kids hung out with other ranch kids--when we could, that is. Timothy Sommers and I ran around together at school or at the fairs, but he lived at the end of the bus route, too far from our ranch to see each other very often."

"Where's he at now?" asked Dale.

Carl replied, "He was drafted into the army and was killed in Vietnam."

"Sorry to hear that," replied Dale.

Carl didn't want to discuss 'Nam, so he commented, "Susan's a nice girl. She wasn't one of the popular girls. Most of the popular girls have kids and have been divorced several times. All they can do is look back at those school days as the best days of their lives--the good ol' days, as they put it. As far as I'm concerned, the good ol' days are right now, ranching with Donna."

Dale was having trouble with his own feelings. Nothing good was said about Carl in town yet he spent days helping Howard rebuild the feed shed and the levy. He wanted to ask Carl about Vietnam, but felt his questions wouldn't be welcome. He also didn't want to spoil his wife's evening and it was obvious she was enjoying her visit with Donna. Dale added, "Susan told me there are several people who don't like to have her wait on them at the café when they come in."

Carl replied, "Susan wasn't one of the class socialites so school wasn't all *rah, rah* wonderful." Carl didn't know how much Susan discussed old school days with Dale but in Carl's mind, they weren't worth remembering. Carl learned long ago to be careful what one said about other people because you never knew who was related or friends with whom. He did add, "Susan and I were probably the lowest on the pecking order in the social order of the class."

As Dale and Carl returned to join the ladies, Donna was telling Susan, "You should come to our place sometime. You both should come. But please be sure to call ahead because we keep the gate locked."

26

STEREOTYPE

Donna while taking a break from her school secretarial work went to visit the faculty room. As she approached, she overheard several of the teachers talking.

"That guy's half-nuts and he never leaves the ranch."

Another teacher interjected, "I'm surprised Donna married him."

A third person commented, "He never attends the county fair. He doesn't go when Sharon--Donna's daughter--is showing her produce either."

The first teacher replied, "My husband told me he's afraid of crowds, just like all of those guys."

Donna didn't go into the room but turned and went back to her desk. She couldn't help feeling sad and upset because Carl would do anything for her and Sharon. He didn't always say much, but most of that was his being self-conscious about his voice.

Donna waited until after the lunch hour before taking a few minutes to return to the staff room to get a cup of coffee. She couldn't dispel the hurt feeling she still harbored.

The idea finally hit her as to why Carl had gotten the part-time job at the auto shop. She never gave it a thought but it was his way of having a job and at the same time, not having to interact with customers. He was good at repairing engines, but he avoided people. She was also aware of his never attending functions where large groups of people would be so those teachers were correct, he never attended a county fair.

Donna got along with most people. She did a good job being the school secretary and wondered where her colleagues got their ideas about Carl. *"Why did they feel the way they did?"*

Her thoughts turned to Sharon; did these people's opinion of Carl contribute to their opinion of Sharon? This was an unsettling notion because Sharon got good grades, worked hard, did well in college, and got along with her peers. Granted, she wasn't one of the popular girls, but she had plenty of friends. One thing she did remember was Sharon's being invited to other people's parties and sleepovers during her younger years but now, she spent most of her time working with the produce and the horses. She was putting applications in for jobs, but none of those had paid off yet. Sharon was a good worker, she'd get hired sooner or later, it would take time though.

27

THE PROPOSAL

1996

Donna happened to glance out the window and saw a Jeep coming down the hill, as it approached, They weren't expecting anybody but since they had to have a key to the gate, it had to be family. The Jeep stopped close to the barn and out of her view so probably went to the barn." She told herself. Donna got an odd sensation and the notion, *Was that Mike? Was he out of the Army or home on furlough? He must have found Carl in the barn.*

Two hours went by and finally she saw Carl and the younger man coming toward the house. As they walked in, Carl informed Donna Mike was home and would be joining them for dinner.

The moment Mike had walked into the barn, he was having second thoughts, was he was doing the right thing or not.

Carl was busy with the horses as Mike approached him.

The first thing Carl asked was, "Are you home on leave or are you out?"

Mike informed him he was officially discharged. The two compared their service experiences and both understood the importance of teamwork in any of the services. Mike told Carl of his humanitarian deployment to Sudan, his deployment to Kuwait, and next to Afghanistan. Though he was involved in some action in Afghanistan, it was the buried roadside bombs that did the most damage. Mike wasn't aware of what Carl had endured in Vietnam, so the two of them had quite a chat.

An hour of visiting went by before Carl asked Mike, "What do you plan on doing from now on?"

"I'm going to try and run the ranch, Dad's no longer able, and Mom is so far behind, she can't keep up. You know Dad can't work anymore with his high blood pressure and heart condition. So many things need repair because in the last two years everything was let go."

Mike changed the topic, "I don't feel I know enough about running a ranch to make a go of it. I'd like to ask if you would be willing to help me?" Mike reiterated how much like in the Army, running the ranch was a team effort and he was in desperate need of a team.

Carl agreed, and after being told Fred wasn't handling any of the ranch business anymore, he said would be willing to work with Mike. Carl told Mike it was getting late so they had better let Donna know she would have one more mouth to feed, so they headed for the house.

During dinner, Donna heard the term *teamwork* used on several occasions and wondered at their connotations. Halfway through dinner, Mike asked Sharon if she would like to help him computerize the ranch's records, yields, animal counts, all the animal statistics, and data and computerize equipment maintenance schedules along with structure maintenance.

Sharon didn't know what to say. She would like to work with Mike but didn't know what reception she would get from the other family members.

Carl waited to see what she would say. She hesitated and looked from her mother to him, he chimed in, "Mike has asked me to help him run the ranch as a team member since he doesn't have much experience, so if you would like to, go ahead, I'm sure you could be a real asset."

Upon hearing this from her father, Sharon quickly said, "Sure, I'd love to."

"One other piece of business," Mike added, "There's absolutely no reason we don't have better communication between the two ranch sections, so I'm going to have a crew out to install a phone line."

After Mike left, the three of them discussed the new ranch management.

Donna's big question was, would Mike be able to run the ranch.

Carl said, "If Mike gets to run it and if he will listen to me, I'm sure he can do it. If he approaches it the way he said, as a team effort, I know he can do it."

Donna didn't say anything but she saw the two ex-servicemen had hit it off and somehow, formed a bond she would never understand. One thing though, she couldn't help being thankful Mike had come back as the Mike she knew, not having endured what Carl had endured.

MIKE PREFERRED to use his motorcycle for getting around the ranch rather than a pickup or his Jeep. This worked well for him since the south half of the ranch wasn't as mountainous as the northern part. On one occasion, he stopped at a small creek where there was a level area of about a half-acre and sat on a rock to get off the bike and think. He was sitting there for thirty minutes before he heard clop, clop, clop, the sound of a horse approaching.

Looking up, he saw Sharon riding her horse down the hill towards him. She rode in, dismounted, and joined him. They talked for a while and they both suggested they meet again at the same location but both were worried what their parents might think. They devised a code so they could phone, and if certain information was requested on the computer, Sharon would know Mike would be able to meet her at this location in secret.

As far as the ranch's computer data, she had everything done as Mike asked. She set up equipment maintenance schedules so the tractor would get certain minor maintenance one month; the next it would be the bigger truck and trailer used for hauling cattle; the month after would be the pickup; and the month, the family car. The system would start all over again.

Since it had been three months since Carl had ridden the fence lines, it was overdue. While riding in the southeast section, he discovered a horse trail veering off and followed a shallow swale towards the southern portion of the ranch. As he followed this trail, he came to an area of a half-acre where a small dam had been built in the creek forming a small pool. He also saw where a campfire had been used.

The area didn't look like any trespassers were camping there, so he continued to search the area. It didn't take long to find a motorcycle trail running up from the lower ranch, so his best guess was Mike was using it as a getaway. A campfire and water in the pond--it all made sense. He also noticed there were a lot of horseshoe tracks in the area also. He decided to backtrack where the horse sign was coming from and discovered it followed the hill to the fence line and the heaviest usage followed the fence in a northern direction. As he followed the tracks north, looking to see if somebody was crossing the fence, he found they turned off and followed the trail to the ranch house. The picture opened and he realized Sharon was meeting Mike at the little pond. He decided to say nothing and continued checking the fence lines. After returning to the house, he didn't speak of it to Donna.

THE POND WAS KNEE DEEP, but they liked to sit on a big rock beside the pond and dangle their feet in the cold water. Mike got a silly notion and pushed Sharon as if he meant for her to go into the water. She lost her balance, fell in, and got soaked. While getting out of the pool, she splashed Mike with as much water as she could before he got too far away. "Why don't you hang your cloths on the bushes and let the sun dry them." Mike suggested.

"Oh wouldn't you love that."

When Sharon got home, she went right to her room to

change. Seeing how disheveled she was. Donna asked, "What happened?"

"I fell," Sharon continued on to her room.

"Not off your horse surely?"

"No," replied Sharon.

On one of the occasions they met, Sharon brought a couple of extra horse blankets so they could sit on them and enjoy a light lunch Mike brought. Mike sat beside Sharon and couldn't think of much except the fact she was driving him crazy. He could faintly detect a kaleidoscope of smells; at one moment, he could detect the earthy aroma of dirt, another moment he could detect the scent of saddle leather and horse. Burying his face in her hair, he could smell her shampoo, and when he kissed her cheek and earlobe, he could detect a soft flowery essence of her perfume. He loved it and couldn't get enough of her company.

Mike taught Sharon how to ride the motorcycle and Sharon taught Mike how to ride a horse. This paid off one day because one of the employees got hurt and radioed in for help. Mike had taken the Jeep into town and while Carl was going to start the truck, Sharon hopped on the bike and roared off with a first aid kit.

Carl watched her go thought, *Wow, she knows how to ride that thing.*

It took time for the ambulance to arrive and get to where the employee was, but Sharon had him comfortable, compression bandages in place, and all the important information needed.

During one of Mike and Sharon's secret meetings, Mike took her in his arms and kissed her. It wasn't the first time he told her he loved her, but finally asked if her mother or father knew of their many meetings.

Sharon said she hadn't told them but wouldn't be surprised if her Dad knew. She didn't know for sure but kind of thought he did. She did tell Mike it would creep her out if her father ever spied on them, and as far as she knew, he didn't. She told Mike if her father ever wanted to, he could get awfully close without them knowing it.

She got that feeling because of what he told her about escaping the prison camp in the jungle. She also told Mike when she arrives home from her rides, her mother often asks where she went or if she enjoyed her ride. She wasn't sure about her father not knowing of their meetings though. He never mentioned it, so it was hard to tell. Her mother often complained she could have used Sharon's help in the garden or around the house though.

Mike also asked her what her mother or father would think about their relationship if it got more serious. Since she was adopted by Mike's cousin, she was a cousin, but her biological father wasn't any relation to the Weston's and neither was her mother. Therefore, she wasn't related by blood to any of them. Sharon admitted it was awkward.

"Right after you went into the Army; I talked to Dad and showed him the necklace you gave me. Dad said it wasn't anybody's business except ours so I don't think it matters to them." Sharon explained.

Though it was fall, the weather was holding. Sharon asked Carl if she could ride the fence line. After several days of explaining what he inspected and prepared her with the tools needed, he allowed her to go. She had already notified Mike, so he met her at their regular meeting place and went with her. They both enjoyed getting away, not to mention having more than an hour or so of alone time.

Sharon left at daybreak, and after meeting with Mike, they worked their way up to the northern boundaries of the ranch. Mike had never seen these portions of the ranch, so this was new country to him. Sharon loved the northern mountainous areas of the ranch because they were covered with large pine forests. It was so different from the lower elevations. It had steeper gullies and the huge rock outcrops.

Sharon had accompanied her dad on several of his

fence inspections, so though not new, it had been several years since she had been in the far corners of the property. They didn't ride hard, and Mike asked Sharon if her mother and father expected her home before nightfall. She said she didn't specifically say she'd be home by dark and certainly wasn't planning on it. She confided they shouldn't be too worried since she was on ranch property and armed. Besides, she had her bedroll with her.

Mike helped her mend a few bad and broken fence areas and they found the small camp spot her dad used. There was grass for the horses and water, so they could have a small fire to cook a small meal and have coffee. They spent a short while sitting against a log looking at the stars and trying to locate and identify the constellations. Mike was sitting on the ground with his back against a log with Sharon sitting in front of him and leaning against him. He had his arms around her, and while kissing her neck, said "I love you."

Sharon liked being in Mike's arms. While sharing a few more kisses, she told Mike she loved him too. They turned in shortly after dark and slept within arm's reach so they could hold hands before they fell asleep. Mike didn't tell Sharon, he wasn't as used to riding as she was, so his whole body ached. Sleep didn't come fast enough.

The next morning after coffee and a small breakfast, they rode to the far northwest corner of the property.

There they stopped and did some target practicing. Mike was darn good with a rifle and was quite pleased with Sharon's shooting.

Mike commented, "Your dad taught you well." Coming from Mike, the compliment pleased her.

Once they rode the complete perimeter of the northern ranch, they returned to their meeting place where Mike rode his bike home and Sharon took the two horses' home. She brushed, fed, and put them in their stalls before she returned to the house with a full report for her dad.

After Sharon left, Carl noticed she took both horses. He seldom took two horses, so he guessed Sharon was going to have company on her fencing trip. He said nothing to Donna, but the second day did hear gunfire that sounded like it came from the far corner of the ranch. He wouldn't have heard it but it was a still morning and nothing was making noise at the time. He hoped Sharon hadn't run into trouble but guessed she wasn't alone. Since he knew of her meetings with Mike, he figured Mike was probably with her. Well no harm in that, but he kept his own council and didn't mention it to Donna.

The following month, Mike visited the upper ranch section and walked into the barn to talk to Carl. Carl was under the tractor and in no mood for small talk.

After asking what was wrong with the tractor, Mike asked if Sharon was his cousin. "Since you're my dad's cousin, and you adopted Sharon, she really isn't related to me, is she? Being adopted, she's a cousin name-wise, but other-wise, we're not related, right?"

Carl was half listening and commented, "If you're going to stand there jabbering with one arm as long as the other, hand me the ¾ inch wrench."

After handing the wrench to Carl, Mike waited for an answer. Carl was trying to get the tractor running before dinner so wasn't in the mood for small talk. The last thing he was expecting was a discussion of any importance.

After a few minutes of silence, Mike asked, "Can I have your blessing to ask Sharon for her hand in marriage?"

It got really quiet under the tractor for a few seconds and finally Carl replied, "Under the circumstances, shouldn't you be asking her mother, but since you asked, you can if she will have your lazy butt."

They both chuckled because Mike was anything but lazy. He had proved that many times after taking on the running of the ranch. Carl crawled out from under the tractor and gave Mike a big hug and said, "You have my blessing."

Two weeks later Sharon and Mike were once more enjoying each other's companionship, sitting on their favorite rock with their feet dangling in the little pond. Mike put his arm around Sharon's shoulder and said, "I love you."

Sharon leaned against Mike so they could kiss and also told him, "I love you."

Mike rose and stepped into the water in front of Sharon and lowered himself to his knees. Sharon instantly thought he was going to grab her and pull her into the water. She had news for him. She was ready to put her feet on his chest and push him backwards.

Mike asked; "Sharon, will you marry me?" as he reached for her hands.

She was taken completely by surprise and jumped off the rock and as he stood up, she threw her arms around him and answered, "Yes, you know I will. It's taken you this long to ask?"

Mike turned red as he slipped the ring on her finger. How right she was. It took time to get the nerve to ask.

During dinner that evening, Sharon announced her engagement to Mike and showed both Donna and Carl the ring Mike had given her. Donna was surprised and from the look on Carl's face, she got the feeling this wasn't news to him.

Sharon observed his lack for surprise but didn't say anything. She remembered their discussion during the horseback ride she asked him to accompany her on.

Carl admitted, "Mike asked me for my blessing two weeks ago. I'm really happy for the two of you. It took him long enough."

"Oh my, what a beautiful ring, Sharon." Donna said as she leaned forward for a closer look. It made hers look old and shabby but it didn't matter; it was still her ring and she cherished every day of her fifteen years with Carl.

Donna got out a bottle of wine and poured a glass for each. "I wish to propose a toast." They raised their glasses as Donna continued, "To Mike and Sharon on their engagement and to their wedding. With your wedding, the two of you will combine the southern ranch and the northern ranch into the same old big ranch it was to begin with."

28

MIKE AND SHARON

1997

JoAnn was shocked at reading the invitation they received. She hadn't paid attention to the name of the sender so the announcement was a total surprise. Her little brother was getting married. It took her several minutes before she realized who Sharon Weston, his bride to be was.

As she handed the invitation to her husband, she exclaimed, "You'll never guess who my brother is marrying! I didn't know he had a girlfriend. Sharon's his cousin; how can he do this?" She sat down and remembered Sharon was not a Weston; she got that name by being adopted by Carl. As she handed the invitation to her husband, she remarked, "Uncle Carl sure knows how to make a mess of things. I can't believe my brother is going to marry Sharon."

JoAnn's husband pointed out that it might be a good thing, being married; the ranch becomes one hundred percent Weston once more.

29

SHARON AND MIKE'S WEDDING

Donna was happy for the two kids. Since Sharon was twenty-five and Mike was twenty-six, they would have ten more years together than she and Carl, who had gotten married when Carl was thirty-six and she was thirty-five. *How can it already be 1996?* She pondered. *It seems like Sharon was starting kindergarten last week.*

Donna was helping Sharon with her wedding planning and commented, "I have something to give you and I'm hoping you will wear it for your wedding."

"What is it Mom?" Donna took the jade necklace from its cloth bag and gave it to Sharon. "That's beautiful Mom, where did you get it?" Donna knew Sharon wouldn't remember it and Donna didn't attend functions where such a special piece of jewelry would be worn so Sharon didn't know she had it. "Carl gave it to me and I wore it on my wedding day. Carl said it's immensely powerful and brings good luck. It brought him back and in his words, met and married me. I want you to have it and I'm not telling Carl. I want it to be a surprise when he sees I gave it to you."

The wedding was held in the local church, and Carl walked Sharon down the aisle. "I see your mother gave you her jade necklace, I hope it brings you the luck and happiness it brought me." The front row seats looked funny with Connie and Fred on one side and Carl and Donna on the other. Donna's brother and his wife sat right behind them. JoAnn and her husband sat behind her mother. One of Sharon's college friends was her maid of honor and Bill was Mike's best man. A number of rancher neighbors attended as did several of Sharon's friends. Six friends of Mike's also attended; including two he served with in the Army.

At the reception, Connie approached Carl and Donna and exclaimed, "I never dreamed this would happen, especially between these two."

Donna replied, "I'm so happy for the two of them. They've always been close and good friends. I pray they will be happy."

Connie replied, "I guess I didn't see this coming but they always were the best of friends." Connie looked at

Carl, and all he did was give her a smile while he thought, *I saw it coming from a mile away; they were meeting secretly years ago. Who took who to the rodeos and accompanied Sharon at every fair?*

JoAnn approached her brother, and while giving both Mike and Sharon a hug, commented, "You sure know how to surprise your sister. I didn't know you were seeing anybody. Well, I will admit, I've been away for a few years, but this came as a complete surprise."

Mike replied, "I hope it's a happy surprise."

JoAnn replied, "It is. I have a little sister I have to get to know now."

30

A DIFFERENT RANCH

1998

As the next five years went by, Mike and Sharon lived in the main ranch house with Mike's mother, Connie. Mike and Sharon slowly took more responsibility for running the ranch, and though Sharon always pictured herself working in town, she discovered there was work enough right at home on the ranch. While Carl helped and suggested how things could be done more efficiently, Mike was such a fast learner and there became less and less work for Carl to do.

Mike taking on more responsibility put Carl in the position of gardener for Donna so they increased the quantity and quality of produce for their roadside stand. Donna was finally able to get Carl to help her with produce displays at the county fair. Carl would help her set up but never attended the fairs. He loathed big crowds and crowded places. Donna was happy when she won several first place awards for her displays. It helped their business at their roadside stand. Donna often took extra orders for farm fresh produce, and if the order was large enough, she would have Carl deliver it with his pickup truck. Otherwise, everything was sold at the roadside stand.

While the produce business thrived, Carl found he was doing more and more while Donna was doing less and didn't have the energy she used to have. During the fifth year, Donna was diagnosed with cancer and slowly got sicker and thinner. It became impossible for her to work in the garden, much less man the roadside stand. It became difficult for Carl to work the garden and take care of Donna. His time with her was growing short and he was going to miss her.

Donna's health slowly deteriorated during the following two years. Near the end, she refused to go to the hospital for more miserable treatment and wanted to stay home. Sharon tried to help, but between helping Mike with the ranch, doing anything with the produce was out of the question. Mostly, it became taking time with Donna to give Carl a chance to take a break and go for a horseback ride someplace. For Carl, it was a privilege to get to ride the fence line, not because he had to, but for his peace of mind.

Donna passed in 2003 and the memorial service was hard for Carl and he wasn't looking forward to the days to follow.

Donna had plenty of friends that she'd made because of the farm stand and quite a few of the school employees attended. Several fellows from the auto shop also attended. Susan and Dale Miller attended and they both approached Carl with their condolences and an invitation to drop by whenever he wished. Carl thanked them but knew he'd never take them up on the offer. He wasn't that comfortable with Dale. Carl couldn't put a finger on it but he felt Dale didn't like him. Talking to him was nothing like talking to Susan's brother Howard. Well, Howard was another Vietnam veteran, and that made all the difference in the world.

Donna's passing took a toll on Carl. He went back to the auto shop on his part-time basis to keep from going crazy. He didn't take care of the garden during the year after Donna's death. He was able to get some produce from it for personal use, but it hurt too darn bad to try and spend any time in it, much less try to care about growing anything in it anymore.

31

JIM

2005

One afternoon the following year while working at the auto shop, a fellow drove in and needed an oil change, wheel bearings packed on his truck, and utility trailer he was towing. This was one of the few days Carl ever entered the front office; as he handed his list of finished work orders to the bookkeeper, he noticed the fellow wearing a ball cap with "Vietnam veteran" embroidered on it. Carl looked at him, nodded, and commented, "We fought the same war."

Carl went back into the shop to work, and after a few minutes, the customer came back and said, "My rig needs some work, and they're going to try and fit me in. I was in the infantry in-country, and you?"

Carl glanced up and replied, "I'm working, but I'll spot you lunch at the cafe two blocks down the street at noon."

"Perfect," was all the fellow said as he departed.

Talking to other veterans was something Carl seldom did, but in this case the fellow's truck and trailer had Alaska license plates, and it piqued his interest.

Carl entered the café and the fellow had already arrived and got a booth for them. He stood up and shook Carl's hand, and introduced himself, I'm Jim from Sitka, Alaska. I'm on my way to New Hampshire to help his sister move to Alaska."

Carl introduced himself, and once they ordered, started comparing war experiences. Carl being a prisoner of war overshadowed anything Jim experienced, and their conversation turned to their treatment upon return. Carl's return was so different since it was years after the war so it didn't compare to Jim's.

"Returning from Vietnam through Los Angeles was terrible. The anti-war mob treated us like dirt at the airport. It didn't matter where I went; I was never made to feel welcome." Jim continued, "None of that crap took place in Alaska. In those small towns everybody knew you. They were either classmates, played on the basketball team with you, played with you as kids, babysat you at one time, or you babysat them, or you were related in some distant way.

In any case, none of the unwelcoming shit was experienced in Alaska. It was, 'Great to see you back, do you have a job yet?' The government promised we'd get our jobs back after our service but they didn't make good on it so it didn't take place. What was your experience?"

"Due to circumstances beyond my control, I returned ten years after the war. Let's just say the family wasn't enthused," Carl replied.

Jim continued, "I suppose I was lucky. In Alaska I was able to get jobs that paid well enough I needed little assistance to get through college. Granted, I didn't attend the most prestigious or expensive colleges either."

"What do you do up there?" Carl asked.

"I fish on a purse seiner, the *Molly Kay*. We fish in the summer and do maintenance on the boat and gear all winter."

They were interrupted when Susan stopped by their table with the coffee pot and asked, "You guys need a refill?"

That broke the moment and Carl knew he had to get back to work, so he replied, "No thank you."

Susan put the bill on the table. Carl put cash down for their lunches and thanked Jim for their time together and wished him well on his trip east.

Jim looked at the size of the tip and asked, "You know her?"

"We went through school together."

Jim thanked him for lunch and they headed back to the auto shop.

By closing time it became apparent Jim's truck and trailer wouldn't be finished. Carl asked him if he made arrangements for the night's stay.

"No," was Jim's reply. "I'm probably going to have stay at the motel."

"If you want, I can save you the trouble and you can stay at my place. I live on a ranch but will be back at work tomorrow, so we both have the same destination. I can save you the cost of a meal and a bed," Carl added with a grin.

Jim jumped on Carl's offer, and later in the evening over coffee, Jim commented, "You're lucky you can take care of this place and still ride the horses. I run out of steam too soon. I'm out of shape, I'm diabetic, and all my joints hurt. I've talked to quite a few other Vietnam veterans, and most of us feel a lot of this is caused by our exposure to Agent Orange. The VA doesn't think so--or won't admit to it--so they won't help us. Damn, some of the guy's I know need help now, not tomorrow."

Carl replied, "I was lucky on that note, I never came in contact with it. Returning after ten years, all I wanted to do was crawl into a hole, and this cabin was perfect. We added the addition after I married my wife because she had a daughter so we needed more room. I moved in during the fall of 79 and the place was perfect, the family didn't find me for two months. Then the shit hit the fan. You could say my cousin went to full general quarters, man all battle stations."

JIM'S TRUCK was finished by 2:00 PM the next day. He was anxious to get started for his sister's, so he said goodbye to Carl, thanked the crew, and drove off. Carl didn't want to bother fixing anything at home so decided to have dinner at the café. Carl's mood brightened up when Susan placed a menu in front of him and asked what he'd like to drink.

32

HELPING A FRIEND

Every Thursday Mike and Sharon would have Carl for dinner at their place so they could keep an eye on him and keep him informed of how the ranch was going. They were both concerned about him since he didn't have any friends to spend time with and didn't go out of his way to make friends. After a few months went by, Carl took to having dinner at the café after work at the auto shop once a week. He always picked a day Susan was waiting tables. She always had a kind word for him or asked about his wellbeing.

It took almost two years for Carl to want to work in the garden so once the weather turned warmer, he tilled it and put it back in grass. Between horseback riding and normal maintenance, Carl only visited the café once a month.

Two years after Donna's death, he was having dinner with Sharon and Mike and they informed him of Dale Miller's death. It was quite sudden, and Sharon let him read the obituary in the newspaper. Dale had had a heart attack and passed away. They weren't able to save him due to the time lag between discovering him and the time they got him to the hospital.

Carl, Mike, and Sharon attended Dale's memorial service, and Carl was saddened to see only a dozen people attended. If it hadn't been for the café crew, there would have been eight people. Several of the people in attendance Carl didn't know.

Carl made it a point to put his arm around Susan's shoulder and tell her, "If you need help with anything, let me know." Susan thanked him, but as he walked away, he thought, *would she ever ask for help? Probably not, but I meant what I said.*

Eight months later, Carl was horseback riding, trying to overcome boredom, loneliness, and his melancholy mood. Carl surprised himself when he found himself riding into Susan's yard. He wasn't sure why he rode over but wanted to check on her to see how she was after losing her husband.

As he approached the house, he could see many little

things weren't getting taken care of. The yard needed care, the banister on the porch needed repair, and it looked like the stockyard area needed attention.

He rode up to the house and started to dismount, Susan stepped out and teased, "You come to sleep in the barn again?" She invited him in and asked if he'd like something to drink.

"Coffee if you have it." Carl replied.

Once seated at her kitchen table, they spent an hour chatting and as he started to leave, he commented, "I think you could use a little help around here. Would you mind if I drive over tomorrow and help you with a few of the repair chores?"

Susan agreed and admitted the ranch was getting away from her and she didn't know where to start, much less what should be taken care of first.

The next day Carl repaired some of the small things around the house and barn. While in the barn, he noticed the area needed cleaning and upkeep. He returned three days in a row and fixed fences, stalls in the barn, mowed the lawn, and fixed the porch railing.

He missed Mike and Sharon's weekly dinner but informed them of his whereabouts. Mike and Sharon had the ranch well under control, so they didn't need Carl's help. He felt like a third wheel at their ranch and sticking around his own place was too painful, so as far as he was concerned; helping Susan gave him something to do.

Carl spent most of the following week working at Susan's but drove home each night. Susan made sure she had a dinner ready for him each evening so he wouldn't have to fix a meal after he drove home.

Thursday of the third week, Carl put in an extra-long day and was exhausted, rather than having him drive home, Susan told him to go upstairs and use the spare bedroom.

Carl's eyes shut the moment his head hit the pillow.

The next morning Susan had breakfast ready at 6:00 AM, and Carl was ready for coffee and anything she put on the table. While eating breakfast, Carl asked Susan how the running of the ranch was going and how the finances were. Granted, they were personal questions, but Susan was candid and explained the place was getting away from her and therefore so was her management of the ranch.

Carl replied, "If you don't mind, would you let me help you?"

Susan replied, "I can't ask a friend to do that."

Carl explained, "Mike and Sharon are running the Weston ranch and have a hired helper who does much of the work so they don't really need me. I'm nothing more than a third wheel. I know ranching, so let me give you a hand."

Susan's reply was, "I'd love to do that, but I can't pay you any wages."

Carl responded, "I don't recall saying anything about wages?"

Susan was surprised at his offer, much less the fact she was getting the help she needed. In her eyes, Carl's help was a godsend; he was getting everything "squared away" as he put it and she had to smile knowing it was one of his Navy-isms.

He made a run into town and gave the auto shop his notice. They thanked him for his help and mentioned he'd be welcome back any time.

After dinner the following evening, Carl asked if he could review the books. "If I'm going to help you, I need to know what is costing you the most and where your profit is coming from."

Susan was reluctant but finally gave in. While she was busy in the kitchen, Carl spent two hours going through the books. Susan finished in the kitchen and came in to check on him, Carl went through the cash flow with her and suggested several changes and explained why the changes should be made.

As the summer wore on and Carl continued to work the Miller ranch for Susan, he spent more and more nights in the spare bedroom. He didn't have much and didn't need much, so it was comfortable. Susan was a good cook, so he wanted for nothing.

By the following year, Carl had the place in tip-top order--"squared away" as he put it--and definitely making a profit. He also suggested working with some Hereford cattle to show at the county fair. If they could win an award, it would help get the Miller ranch name in the paper. It would be nice to get some recognition to bolster your livestock value at auction.

Carl also explained to Susan the reason for choosing Herefords. They eat less pasture grass and feed per animal than other breeds while turning it into prime beef and they do well in Montana's climate. You're limited on the quantity of cattle you can feed due to the size of your range. Herefords don't bring the same price as Angus but they are still a prime animal and command a good price.

One morning at breakfast, Carl got up to refill his coffee mug and, on his way back--didn't even know why he did it--set his cup on the table and gave Susan a brief shoulder message.

"Thank you, that felt good," was Susan's reply.

Several days later while she was putting things away in

the kitchen, Carl walked up behind her and gave her a hug as he thanked her for dinner.

Carl was as surprised as she was. Carl wondered to himself, *What's getting into me? How is it that somehow Susan's creeping into my heart?*

Susan was a bit surprised Carl took her hand, but she liked the idea of him liking her. She had to admit, he was hard to get to know since he didn't talk much, and when he did, it was all business. He surprised her that day in the kitchen when he hugged her. She had no idea he was going to do that. It felt really good though. The feeling you have a friend who did as much as Carl did for her was pure happiness and such a blessing.

Carl was basically Susan's ranch manager, and she was happy he had turned the place around. It was going downhill since Dale had passed away but she didn't know what to do to change the situation.

She was afraid she'd eventually lose the ranch and, with it, her home. Carl knew what to do and though he would explain problems to her, she didn't always grasp them.

She was relying on Carl more and more. He had Sharon purchase a computer so she could computerize the books the same as what Mike had done at their ranch. It made bookkeeping so much easier, and the programing included graphs so costs, profits, and problem areas were easier to spot.

On one of the days Sharon was working with the computer, she went upstairs to use the bathroom. She felt guilty for spying but sneaked a peek into the two bedrooms. She could see her dad was using the spare room. Sharon felt guilty for snooping because it wasn't any of her business. So what if Susan and Carl were sleeping together? He was obviously living with her anyway. Sharon wasn't surprised because she knew her dad was lonely.

The one detail she didn't know was Susan's fear of being alone in her advanced years. Being shunned as a child hurt but being alone later in life frightened her. The possibility of losing her home was terrifying.

THE TIME CAME to have some of the animals slaughtered, Carl was busy seeing to each animal, making sure of the weights, and making sure the meat was properly taken care of. He was so tired; he ate his meal, took a shower, and went to bed.

Sometime in the middle of the night, he was vaguely aware of Susan crawling in beside him. He was too exhausted to react and went back to sleep.

Waking the next morning, he was surprised to find Susan's back to him yet pressed against him, and all he could see was a mass of her coal-black hair. *How am I going to get up without waking her? This isn't going to be easy because I also have my arm around her.* He had another busy day ahead, so he needed to get going. As he gently pulled his arm from around her, she woke and turned to face him.

Carl couldn't help himself; their closeness could be measured in inches so he kissed her.

The kiss was returned and after several kisses, Carl commented, "I suppose I'm going to have to put the coffee on and go without breakfast."

Susan giggled and the two of them got up. Carl had coffee on by the time Susan came downstairs in her pajamas.

While Carl drank his coffee, he watched Susan fix breakfast. He was aware of every move she made and thought, *Dang if I'm not falling in love with her. She sure knows how to drive me crazy and get right into my heart.* He finished his breakfast and was ready to leave, he gave her a hug and kissed her, first the top of her head, next her neck, and by this time Susan turned and returned his kisses.

Carl commented, "You're creating all kinds of

problems by cavorting around in front of me in your night duds."

"Am I now?" was Susan's reply.

Susan was confused since Carl didn't take advantage of her sleeping next to him. She was glad he stayed on task and took care of the ranch first, but how did she feel? Was she hurt because he didn't respond the way she expected or was she happy he didn't take advantage of the opportunity she offered? She didn't know what to think or how to react to Carl's *We have business to attend to, so do I have to put the coffee on?* attitude. Was he teasing her or was he pushing her away?

She didn't know.

She wasn't sure how she felt about herself much less why she joined him in his bed. She wasn't sure why she did it. In a way, she was glad it turned out the way it did, but what if it hadn't? She couldn't imagine how she would feel. Why was she acting like a silly schoolgirl?

I hope I'm not being foolish but I love Carl; Oh darn, I'm sorry Dale, I loved you. I'm not trying to be a traitor or a cheater. I need Carl, I want him, and I love him. I pray you understand. "Please understand if it weren't for Carl, I was going to lose the ranch and my home." she said out loud.

Making sure she didn't do that again, she always slept in her own room, but Carl always made it a point to kiss her goodnight. He also kissed her before he left after breakfast.

She always had breakfast ready at 6:00 AM and Carl was never late. On one of the slower work days, Carl and Susan sat on the front porch enjoying the warm evening while Carl sipped his coffee.

Taking Susan's hand, Carl said, "I don't know what you did or how you did it, but I enjoy being with you. I've discovered I love you."

Susan squeezed his hand and with a big smile replied, "I love you too."

What he didn't tell her was while she fixed breakfast in her pajamas, she looked too damn good to him. Looking at Susan, he saw a hard working woman who treated others with kindness. She treated him different than most other people. He liked her so enjoyed helping her where he could. Granted, the whole thing was spiraling out of reason. *One day I was out riding and stopped by to see how she was doing, ended up living with her and now, I want to stay with her.*

She never bad-mouthed other people, especially those who treated her badly in the past, she put them aside and got on with life. Carl liked that about her.

While eating dinner, Susan showed Carl the mail and commented, "This is an invitation to our fiftieth class reunion. I'll bet you got one too."

Carl asked, “Are you going to go?”

“No,” replied Susan, “Why should I go so they can hug me and lie while saying how happy they are to see me after those years of teasing they put me through?”

Carl agreed one hundred percent and commented, “I understand. I had to thrash every ball player, so I'm sure they'd love to see me. What the hell, if we attended together, I bet we'd create quite a stir. I'd probably end up breaking Deric's nose again.”

After that remark, Carl went on to tell Susan about the day Deric and his three friends drove their motorcycles and four-wheelers onto his property and threatened Donna. “It sure popped their balloon when Pete Holcomb's bike blew up.”

Susan replied, “I heard a rumor about it at the café, something about you destroying someone's property and the Sheriff was looking into it. What did the sheriff do?”

Carl replied, “Oh yes, he caught up with me at the auto shop, questioned me, and later came to the ranch. But nothing ever came of it because of their trespassing and cut the fence.”

Later that night, Carl dreamt he was operating the sampan for Chi Lou Mei while trying to look inconspicuous so the harbor patrol authorities wouldn't stop them. The dream evolved into him helping Donna in the garden and preparing the produce. As he woke, his mind was troubled after being with Donna in his dream but now with Susan.

Damn, he'd never get back to sleep, so he went downstairs and made coffee. Carl walked out onto the porch with his mug of coffee and let his mind go wild. He couldn't believe what life had handed him. He'd never looked at it from the standpoint of three women making such an impact on his life.

Chi Lou Mei saved his life and got him to Singapore where he got on the freighter for San Francisco. Donna was the love of his life and gave him a family. Susan was becoming a loving companion who he wanted to spend more time with.

Carl pondered, Susan was genuinely nice, considerate, and damn, he couldn't take his eyes off her the morning while she was in her pajamas. Carl had to smile because most people would consider pajamas as overly modest and not sexy at all. Seeing Susan in her pajamas and her long black hair made Carl overly aware of her presence and looks. Dang, he couldn't get enough of her, he wanted her, but there was work to do and that picture wouldn't leave his mind's eye.

33

ERIC

2013

Though Susan and Carl hadn't paid any attention, a month had gone by since their class reunion.

Sunday afternoon at 2:00 PM a car parked in front of the house. Susan heard the car doors slam shut and reached the door just as a couple were about to knock on the door.

Susan answered the door with a "Hello?"

The man explained, "You didn't come to our class reunion, and I was wondering how you were doing. I haven't seen you since Dale's service."

The man introduced himself as Eric Crossman, who Susan recognized because she often waited on him in the café. He went on to introduce his wife, "This is my wife, Dawn. We met at college and got married after graduation."

"Won't you come in?" replied Susan as her mind went into "on guard" while wondering what brought them to the ranch.

While this was taking place, Carl walked from the office and joined them.

Susan turned to him and commented, "This is Eric Crossman and his wife Dawn. You probably don't remember him, but he was in our class."

Susan explained to the couple, "You probably don't remember my friend, Carl Weston," as she indicated Carl beside her.

Susan turned back to Dawn and asked, "Can I get you anything to drink?"

Carl interjected, "Coffee's on."

They followed Susan into the kitchen dining room while she got cups and some glasses for those who wanted a cold drink.

Carl commented, "Have a seat," while motioning to them to have a seat at the table.

Susan brought the drinks to the table and said, "I didn't get a chance to thank you for coming to Dale's service. I appreciated it."

After some small talk, Eric commented, "I always

admired you because your grades were always so much better than mine. School was a real struggle for me, and I could never do as well as you did."

Carl couldn't remember Eric and waited for him to announce the reason for their visit. Eric couldn't remember Carl, and since Carl's face was changed, there wasn't any way to recognize him.

Eric heard many rumors concerning Carl so wasn't sure how to handle the situation, much less what to say.

Carl couldn't remember this person, so he commented, "School days weren't all *rah-rah* wonderful, so I've forgotten many of those people. In the Navy, your life depended on your shipmates so you worked as a team. There are damn few things more important than one's shipmates while at sea. You and your shipmates depend on each other to keep their ship afloat, come hell or high water. Those are the people I remember."

Eric replied, "Susan and I used to be band students, so we didn't hang out with most of the other students. Neither one of us was popular. In any case, a few of us are trying to form a small alumni band and want you to join us if you would. Maybe there would be some camaraderie there too. It would be nice to be able to possibly play at the fair or something, you know?"

Susan still had her flute but hadn't played in years. She certainly wasn't into being ridiculed or teased, so she wasn't going to commit to Eric's suggestions. She was also reserved concerning his suggestions, knowing he was one of the only two boys to ever take her on a date. That hadn't ended well either.

Eric looked at Carl and commented, "She could play her flute one heck of a lot better than I could play my saxophone."

At his comment about her not being one of the popular kids, Susan interjected, "I was Miss Goody-Two-Shoes, so I found myself on the sidelines most of the time." It was the nicest way she could describe her being shunned by her classmates.

Eric replied, "Yes, I remember, you were standoffish and always wore those funky dresses. One thing though, you didn't date much so didn't end up like so many of the girls--divorced with several kids by several different husbands."

Susan's mind took her back to those days when her mother always made her dresses to ensure she was dressed modestly and the incessant teasing she received. Granted, her mother made them at least two inches longer than any other girls, and her blouses were always cut high. Her father didn't earn a lot of money, so her mother always made sure she stretched it as far as she could.

She also remembered the one date she went on with

Eric; he took her to a movie and to a secluded place and parked. She wasn't into heavy necking and wanted to go home.

Eric added, "You might not have been the class champion, but you were always nice to people, and much like me, you married somebody from out of town. School and growing up wasn't always easy, but you always seemed to do so well. Dale was from another town, so you also broke the 'small town syndrome' as I like to call it. I did too; Dawn's from Chadron, Nebraska. We met at college together." Eric glanced at Carl and thought *I don't remember him from our classes, but what the hell happened to him?* Rumor has it *he's a crazy Vietnam veteran, robbed the ranch from the Weston's, destroyed Pete Holcomb's bike, and now he's living with Susan. Good God, what does she see in him? She was the girl* ***who*** *never did anything wrong.* Eric continued, "Anyway, we've got to be going, I remembered you in school and since you didn't attend the reunion, I wanted to stop by and see how you're doing. Anyway, please think about the band we're trying to organize."

Susan saw them to the door and thanked him for being concerned. After they left, she turned to Carl and said, "I wasn't expecting that."

Carl replied, "I think he had a crush on you back in school?"

Susan looked at him and retorted, "The boys didn't give me a second look much less like me."

Carl looked at her and replied, "He did, you didn't know it. I'd also say he's done a lot of growing up since those days. It's more than I can say for some of our other classmates."

CARL DIDN'T LIKE to have to go into town, but sometimes necessity forced him to run errands. This particular day he stopped in at the feed store. Deric was sitting in his pickup nearby. While Carl was on his way into the store, Deric called Carl and commented, "I hear your living with Susan Miller. Which one of the two of you has to wear the paper bag over your head at night?"

Carl wanted to rearrange Deric's face but replied, "I see you like to ride your four-wheeler in the hill country east of our northern boundary. Be careful in that area because some of those ATVs and motorcycles have electrical problems and it ignites their gas tanks. I'd hate for somebody to be riding one of those things and have it happen, somebody could get hurt."

"You bastard, are you threatening me?" was Deric's response as he hit the gas pedal and sped out of the parking lot.

Carl smiled to himself, knowing Deric would be forever looking over his shoulder and wondering, is Carl drawing a bead on his four-wheeler or not. Planting the seed of possible retribution in Deric's brain was enough for Carl.

Call it mental warfare if you will.

34

SUSAN'S DAY

While sitting on the porch enjoying coffee and the large October harvest moon, Carl took Susan's hand in his. They weren't talking much, though enjoying each other's company and the peaceful, quiet solitude.

After several minutes, Carl asked Susan, "Are you happy the way the ranch has been operating? Is there anything I haven't taken care of?"

Susan replied, "I couldn't be happier how everything is going."

Carl commented, "I've enjoyed my time with you and working the ranch. I want to continue on this path but I need to know how you feel. You've captured my heart, and I love you."

Susan took her time before answering. *Was he was*

suggesting they continue living together with him running the ranch for her? Was he suggesting the same arrangement but with benefits? She wouldn't tolerate the last so where was Carl going with this?"

Carl continued, "I want to spend all of my time with you." As he said this, he released her hand, moved to stand in front of her and asked, "Will you marry me?"

Susan wasn't expecting this. "Yes." She loved him and didn't want him leaving her. She also liked his running the ranch and their mornings and evenings together. He was also always on her mind, so yes, she wanted him to be her husband. She could now rest her mind, she often worried he'd never ask. He was her best friend, and she definitely never wanted to be alone. "Yes, and I love you too, Carl," she added as he pushed a ring on her finger.

He pulled her up from her chair and squeezed her to him and gave her a big kiss, which she returned. Susan's mood went from enjoying a quiet evening to being so happy she was beyond words.

A moment later, Susan took her seat, Carl was still standing, looking at her and not knowing what to say or add, reached for her coffee mug and his own and said, "I'll get us some refills," and he left to refill their coffee mugs.

Returning and handed Susan her coffee mug, she replied, "Thank you, you don't know how happy you've made me. I love you very much." As she looked down into her lap, she mumbled, "I was afraid you'd never ask ugly ol' me to be your wife."

Carl once more took her hand and squeezed it and replied, "You're not ugly, and you have a heart of gold. I'm getting the better of the deal because I know what I look like." He also added with a frown, "I also know what I sound like."

They both squeezed each other's hand. At sixty-nine, neither one of them was getting any younger.

The next morning while drinking their second cup of coffee, Susan asked, "Where should we get married, and who should we invite?"

Carl replied, "We can have it any place you wish. Who would you like to invite?" Carl asked this last knowing neither one of them had a long list of friends.

Susan replied, "I want my brother Howard to walk me down the aisle, and I'm going to ask your daughter Sharon if she'll be my bridesmaid."

Carl looked at her and commented, "Looks like you have everything planned already

Susan had to ask, "Who do you want as your best man?"

Carl took a few minutes before replying, "Probably Mike."

Susan added, "Would you mind if we got married right here on the ranch?"

Carl replied, "Sounds good to me. Our Lord will be with us, our families will be with us, our few friends will be with us, and this place will be our home. What better place to get married?"

Susan could have hugged him and kissed him a thousand times because she felt exactly the same.

The following Sunday they both slept in, but Carl reached the kitchen first and put on the coffee. Susan, still wearing her pajamas, joined Carl with a first cup of coffee. As Susan started breakfast, Carl crossed the room and put his arms around her. He ran his hands up to her shoulders and gave her a squeeze and moved his hands slowly down her back. While kissing her he slowly moved his hands to her shoulders but this time, under her pajama top.

An hour later they came back downstairs, refilled their coffee mugs. Susan finally asked Carl with a smile, "What got into you?"

Carl replied, "You've been putting a pinch of love in my morning coffee every day and it finally took effect. Besides, I've told you what you do to me when you cavort around here in your pajamas."

"You're impossible. I'm not pretty, my hair isn't combed yet, and these old pajamas aren't sexy," Susan said.

Carl replied, "You don't know what I see, and as far as I'm concerned, you're everything I could ever want."

THE WEDDING WAS simple and small. Susan had a difficult time finding a minister who would officiate because they didn't attend any of the local churches. Carl definitely wanted a minister so God would be present. Vietnam left a stain on his soul but God brought him back home. God preserved his Aunt Carol till he was back. God gave him Donna for a wife. God gave him the blessings he'd had. Yes, like he had in Vietnam, he wanted God at the wedding. Nothing else mattered, who attended, where it was held, nothing else mattered.

Mike was Carl's best man, and Sharon was Susan's bridesmaid. Susan let her hair hang straight down, and its black color showed off well with her long white dress. She also wore a cobalt blue beaded necklace because it belonged to her great-grandmother who emigrated from Russia. JoAnn, her husband, and William also attended. Susan's friends at the café attended, as did the fellows from the auto shop. The ceremony was held on the ranch in the early spring. In Carl's eyes, it was a new year, a new life, a new beginning. What he didn't vocalize was, *God has given me a new blessing, one I'll cherish to the end of my days.*

After the ceremony, Susan had arranged for a small reception and light snacks to be available, along with coffee, tea, and punch. The small gathering of friends and relatives gave everybody time to socialize and re-establish connections.

JoAnn caught Mike by himself for a moment and asked if Carl held the titles to the Weston Ranch. She continued, "If he does, I'm sure you know if he were to pass, everything would go to his new wife, Susan. You would end up with nothing so if you haven't taken care of this, you'd better see to it soon."

Mike was dumbfounded by JoAnn's concern since she couldn't care less how the ranch was run. Was she interested in his well-being or was her husband hoping to someday get a cut of an inheritance? Mike gave her a quizzical look and replied, "Oh yeah, I'll have to look into it."

Mike knew he didn't have to worry about it because Carl had taken care of this shortly after he started working at Susan's but Mike wasn't going to tell his sister or her husband. *If she loses sleep over it, so what?*

The ranch was definitely profitable, and anytime Carl felt unsure of his management, he contacted Mike and Sharon for their suggestions. Sharon computerized the ranch book keeping like the Weston ranch and showed Susan how the computer system operated so she could do it on a small laptop.

While taking care of the ranch, Carl also took time to teach Susan to ride horses. Every chance he got; he would take her riding. At first it was for an hour in the corral getting her used to the horses. After several months, he took her to the pastures and fields to ride in non-confined areas. As time passed, Carl would take her with him when he was working, and while riding, he could explain parts of the ranch and why he was doing what. Since horses walk slower than motorized vehicles, it was easier to look for predators--four-legged, two-legged, or no-legged ones, like biological predators in the form of disease or noxious weeds that can sicken cattle. While on horseback, it was easier to view the cattle and check for health problems where he could.

After one such ride, they returned the horses to the barn, the two dismounted and where so close, Susan took Carl in her arms and started kissing him. Carl kissed her back and commented, “I’m getting the idea you’re ready for a roll in the hay with me.”

Susan loved his silly banter, but just in case he was serious--she was never totally sure if he was teasing, flirting, or serious--commented with a smile, “Forget that, you’d be all week picking hay from of my hair, and you still have these two horses to brush and feed before dinner.”

35

THE FIRE

In the middle of the night Carl heard the animals making more noise than usual and climbed out of bed to see what was taking place.

The barn was on fire.

He quickly woke Susan and called 911 to report the fire. By the time the fire crew arrived, the barn was a total loss. Miraculously the animals got out but the barn was used more as a repair shop and garage for equipment than for animals.

The following night, exhausted, and sleeping after the long night and day, Carl dreamt of the time he discovered Chi Lou Mei wasn't heading south towards Singapore but north, back into Cambodian waters and into a village they previously visited and instantly panicked. *Why are we back in Cambodia? Is she trying to get rid of me by conveniently having somebody recognize me and turning me in? If I am discovered, I'll never get back to the states and home.* That moment of panic set off a furious and difficult discussion with Chi Lou Mei. It wasn't a comforting feeling until he finally understood why she wouldn't take her boat across the Gulf Of Thailand but instead would circle it by way of Cambodia, Thailand, and finally, Malaysia.

Carl woke drenched in sweat; shaking, and trembling. Susan awoke, while looking at him with a questioning expression wondering what happened and if he was okay. He mumbled something to Susan, and went downstairs. He fixed coffee because he wasn't going to sleep another wink. After that dream, he didn't want to take a chance on another bad dream.

THREE WEEKS later the sheriff dropped by and informed both Carl and Susan the barn fire looked like arson.

Carl remarked, "Who would do that?"

The sheriff replied, "You have quite a bit of insurance on it, so it looks to me like you want to cash in on the insurance."

"Susan had two people make offers on the land but has since informed them she didn't want to sell." replied Carl

"From my sources, the ranch is going downhill and the

bank suggested selling it before they foreclosed on it. The two of you have good reason to try and get the insurance money from it." the sheriff remarked.

Carl responded, "What you hear in town are people's opinions, and most of those are usually wrong since none of them know any of the facts. I question your sources and I'm sure your investigation will find the culprit or discover it was something else we're not aware of."

"Carl, I know my job, and I believe the two of you are trying to collect on this. It won't be the first time someone's tried it."

Carl retorted, "If you do a thorough investigation and find what took place, you'll find the truth unless you're taking money for the judgment you're trying to push on us."

The Sheriff frowned and snapped back, "You veterans sure know how to piss a person off. I take my job seriously, and I intend to get to the bottom of this. I take exceptional affront from you're suggesting I take bribes."

Carl replied, "Most of us veterans are just brutally honest and call it as we see it. You suggested we set the fire to collect on the insurance. I'm suggesting you might be taking money to make that determination."

All this time, Susan's hands were covering her mouth in shock ever since the sheriff first suggested it.

The sheriff went on, "I understand the ranch has been losing money, so I'm sure you're in a bind."

Carl interjected, "Who said we're losing money?"

The sheriff didn't want to answer the question, so commented, "Unless you can prove you weren't losing money, I have to go with my sources."

Carl asked one more time, "Who said we're losing money?"

Carl and Susan had an independent bookkeeping firm go through their ledgers and records to prove the ranch was actually making a profit and able to meet all their bills and mortgages.

Eventually, the Bureau of Farms and Ranches reviewed the case along with the structure and determined the cause to be faulty wiring installations that predated the Millers' ownership.

36

RACHEL

It was getting into the late afternoon and Carl was driving into town. As he neared the area where Donna used to have their produce stand, he slowed as he saw a car parked there with steam coming from under the hood. He pulled in to see if he could help.

The car had an out-of-state license and a young woman of approximately thirty sitting in the car. She lowered her window a few inches as he asked, "Looks like you need some help?"

The hood was raised, so he walked to the front of the car and could see the steam was coming from a hole in the radiator. He returned to the driver side of the car and commented, "You're not driving this thing any farther so can I give you a lift into town?"

"No thank you. I'm going to try and get a tow truck to help me, but thanks."

Carl replied, "At this hour, you're not going to get a tow truck tonight. It's getting dark and you don't want to spend the night here."

She was getting agitated while she was trying to get contacts with her newfangled hand-held phone. He added, "My daughter has one of those things, and she always made calls from over there," as he indicated an area fifty feet away.

Carl walked back to the truck and wrote his home phone number and the name *Susan* on a piece of paper. He took it back to the girl's car and handed her the note and told her, "Call this lady. Her name's Susan and I'm sure she will help you or get help for you."

He returned to his truck and watched the young lady get out of her car and walk to the area Carl had indicated to make the call, all the while watching Carl's pickup.

While she was on the phone, Susan asked her to describe the vehicle the man was driving. After the short description, Susan knew it was Carl who had stopped to help but told the lady she would come and get her. The lady glanced at Carl and brought the phone to him and said, "Susan wants to talk to you."

Susan asked for more information and Carl informed

her of the lady's concern of getting out of her car, much less having him take her to town.

Carl handed the phone back and the lady said, "Susan's going to come and get me so you don't have to stay. Thank you so much for stopping."

She returned back to her car to wait.

The lady waited in her car and Carl waited in his truck. Twenty-five minutes later, Susan pulled in and introduced herself to the lady and told her she would take her where she would be safe rather than having her stay with the car. "You better get any overnight things you might need, too."

The lady grabbed her purse and a small overnight bag she had and got into Susan's car. Susan walked over to Carl's pickup. Carl explained, "I'll get Mike to help me load her car on the trailer and I can take it to the shop tomorrow."

The lady saw Susan talk to the man in the pickup and wondered what they were talking about. Susan returned and while buckling her seat belt said, "I told him he could leave now since I'm taking you to my place where you will be more comfortable than in town."

As Susan drove to the ranch, the lady asked, "Isn't the town in the other direction?"

Susan replied, "Yes, if you want to stay at the hotel and eat at the café, you can but, you will be much more comfortable if you come to the ranch. Besides, it's closer, and I'll bet you're hungry, and I have dinner ready."

At this time the young lady had a meltdown. Tears ran down her cheeks, and she became fidgety and began to shake.

Susan reached over and put her hand on her shoulder and asked, "What's the matter? You're safe, and we will take care of your car in the morning. What's your name?"

Through her tears and her shaking hands, the lady blubbered, "Rachel. That man scared me; I was so frightened, I was afraid to get out of my car."

Susan asked, "What did the man say to you?"

She replied, "It wasn't that-- he looked so mean, and his voice--I've never heard anything like it."

Susan replied, "His name is Carl, he lost his voice while a prisoner of war in Vietnam."

"Why does he still wear that hat?" Rachel asked.

"You'd have to ask him." replied Susan.

As Susan let Rachel into the house, she asked her if she'd like something to drink--coffee, tea, or something cold?

Rachel answered with, "I don't know, I'm not myself right now."

Susan told her she could go upstairs, and at the end of the hall was the spare bedroom where she could collect herself and get ready for dinner.

After a few minutes, Rachel came back downstairs and Susan had her sit at the table and once more asked if she'd like something to drink.

Rachel became less agitated with a cup of hot tea and while seated at the table saw a pickup pull into the yard. She didn't get a good look at the truck, but she was incredibly surprised to see her car on the trailer being pulled by the truck. A second shock hit her when the man who stopped to help her, came walking into the house. She watched him give Susan a kiss, and immediately grab a coffee mug and pour himself some coffee.

With his coffee, he came to the table, sat across from Rachel, and said, "We meet again. I couldn't leave your car out there on the roadside; we'll get it into town tomorrow. I'm Carl by the way, and you are?"

"Rachel McConner," she replied as she assessed the man.

She wasn't so sure she liked him since he didn't remove his hat at the table, and it reminded her of some of her grandpa's friends. The look he gave her while he took several sips of his coffee made her cringe inside, his eyes were so intense. Rachel was relieved after he left the table and he hung up his jacket and hat on his way to bathroom to wash. Susan was putting dinner on the table.

During dinner, Carl explained he would take her car into the shop tomorrow, but they might not be able to get to it right away. Also, if she wished, she was welcome to use their phone to contact anyone she wanted.

Partway through dinner Carl asked, "By any chance are you related to a Kyle McConner?"

RACHEL SAW that strange intense look in Carl's eyes again as she replied, "Yes, that's my grandpa's name, why?"

Carl answered, "I was a prisoner of war with a fellow by that name."

Rachel replied, "I wouldn't know anything about that; though my grandpa was in Vietnam."

"Where's he at now?" Carl asked.

"I don't know; I haven't seen him in two years. He's a truck driver, and between attending college in Minnesota and working summers at Yellowstone, I haven't been back home."

Carl went on and asked, "Most people take the interstate to the north of us. Why did you take the longer rout, our rural state highway?"

Rachel replied, "I've taken the interstate several times and I think my grandpa drives this one quite often, so I wanted to see what it was like."

The following day while taking Rachel's car into town, Carl took advantage of their being alone in the truck and asked, "If you haven't seen your grandfather for two years, where does he live?"

She replied, "He's on the road a lot because after he and grandma got divorced, he started driving trucks. I don't recall any of the particulars, but Dad and Grandma told me he wasn't the same person after he got back from Vietnam. He did some real strange things and Grandma couldn't live with his craziness. I don't know what took place. Dad died in a motorcycle accident, and I didn't like living with Mom and the drunk she married, so when I was in seventh grade, I moved in with Grandpa till I graduated."

Rachel went on, "I sure have to thank you for doing this for me. I don't know what I'd have done if you and Susan hadn't rescued me."

Carl pulled the trailer and car to the back of the auto shop and had the shop crew help him get it off the trailer. After they looked at the car, Rachel was informed they would have to order a new radiator, which would come the next day, so they would either have the car ready the following evening or by the end of the next day.

Carl commented, "Looks like you're with us for another day or two."

Carl dropped by several other places, including the feed store to ask questions, with the comment to Rachel, "I'll be but a minute."

As he left her sitting in the truck, he went in to make inquiries. He was interested in what trucking companies made what deliveries and who the drivers were. He also wanted to know what time each trucker would be driving through and making deliveries.

THE NEXT DAY Carl and Rachel left the ranch at noon to head in to get her car. As they neared the wide spot where the produce stand had been, Carl slowed and pulled into the spot.

Carl keyed his CB and spoke, "Kyle McConner, got your ears on?"

After he repeated this three times, Rachel looked at him with an odd expression, *Has he lost his mind. Why is he calling my grandpa?* she questioned.

Carl had been informed at the feed-lot that Kyle would be making a delivery at approximately 2:00 PM, so he was going to try and make contact so he could meet the man he had escaped from the Viet Cong prison camp with. Carl had to repeat the request frequently because his call wouldn't be picked until the truck got within a certain range.

After repeating he called a dozen times, they received a reply, "Who's calling?"

Carl keyed the mic and replied, "Carl Weston, good buddy. I'm parked at mile post 134.5 at a large wide area off the road. You will see a Ford pickup parked there."

A truck driver will never stop unless he's convinced the call warrants it. In order to jar the trucker into knowing exactly who he was, Carl recalled the nickname they called the prison camp--Dung Ho Pit--as a sarcastic spoof of the gung ho spit-and-polish of the Navy. The prison camp was anything but spit-and-polish. So he replied, "Remember the Dung Ho Pit?"

Silence, there wasn't a reply.

Rachel was looking at him, *"What was he doing? What was he saying?* Nothing made sense.

A few minutes later, an eighteen-wheeler crested the hill, and while taking on the straight stretch of road, black smoke belched from the truck's twin stacks as the driver shifted gears. As the eighteen-wheeler semi-tractor and trailer approached, slowing and pulled off onto the gravel widened area accompanied by two sharp blasts on its air horn while it pulled to a stop.

Carl was out of the pickup and walking towards the truck as the driver climbed down.

The two men give each other a huge hug.

Rachel jumped from the pickup and as she ran around the front of the pickup shouted, "Grandpa!"

Kyle released Carl and grabbed Rachel as she came

into his grasp and they hugged each other. Kyle's ball cap had *Vietnam Veteran* embroidered on it. He was also wearing a denim vest and a big silver chain and cross hanging on his chest. Carl was cognizant of every veteran having their own way of coping with life. Each and every one was marked--not on the outside, but on the inside.

Kyle looked at Carl and said, "I need to know the rest of this story, but I also know it's too long for this stop since I have a schedule to make."

Carl handed him a sheet of paper and said, "My name, rank, and serial number. I want to hear from you in the near future," as he handed him the note with his address and phone number on it. "I rescued this young lady the other day and discovered who she was. We're on our way into town to get her car; she needed a new radiator."

Kyle quickly jotted down his information on a notepad and gave it to Carl. He gave Rachel one more hug and said, "I have to go, I have a schedule I have to keep."

Rachel buckled her seatbelt and with a shocked happy expression she asked, "How did you know?"

Carl gave her a big grin and reached over and squeezed her shoulder.

After they went five miles, Rachel asked, "What was that Gung Ho Pit about?"

Carl looked at her and replied, "That's what we called the Viet Cong prison camp. I knew your grandpa would know absolutely no other person would ever make that comment except me. We escaped together."

Rachel asked, "You were prisoners of war?"

Carl gave her an odd look and replied, "You didn't know?"

Rachel replied, "I lived with Mom until I was in seventh grade. I hated the man she married after Dad died. As far as I know, my grandparents got divorced shortly after Grandpa got back from Vietnam. Dad said Grandpa was a changed man after the war and Grandma couldn't stand him anymore. I couldn't stand my stepdad, so I ran away and lived with Grandpa till I started college. Grandpa didn't talk about it. All I know is Dad said he was a different person when he returned. Grandpa always hung around with other veterans, and Grandma didn't like them. After Dad died, Mom started drinking a lot, and the guy she married was a real drunk. He was repulsive, so I hated to be near him."

Carl interjected, "Your grandpa couldn't have been too bad to have been able to keep you for your last six years of school. I'm surprised your mom didn't file for your return since she obviously had legal custody of you."

Rachel replied, "Mom didn't care as long as Don, my stepfather, kept her in booze. If you didn't notice, Grandpa's a little religious."

Carl commented, "You've heard the old saying, 'there's

no atheists in a fox hole,' and you know where your grandpa was."

Rachel spent the next few minutes quietly looking straight ahead, absorbed in her own thoughts. She was silent for a few minutes, suddenly covering her face with her hands exclaimed, "Oh my God, now I know why grandpa always flew that black flag in front of our house, the one with POW-MIA written on it. I always thought it was so ugly," she said as tears ran down her face.

At 4:00 PM Rachel got her car back and drove it back to Carl and Susan's. She would spend the night and leave in the morning for her drive to Seattle. The next morning after breakfast, she gave both Susan and Carl a big hug and thanked them for all they did for her. She commented, "Nobody has ever done as much for me as you and Susan have. I'm so thankful."

Susan replied, "You've been living in the city too long."

37

KYLE

Memorial Day Weekend

Kyle McConner arrived to spend Memorial Day weekend with Carl and Susan. Kyle was still wearing the same ball cap and vest he had on the day they first met him. He was also wearing the silver chain and cross necklace, so Carl guessed he only took it off at night. He probably wore it every day. The first evening was spent making introductions and filling Susan in on the fact they met in the prison of war camp and escaped together. Carl explained to Kyle how he moved onto the Weston ranch and used Kyle's name for months before being discovered. He also explained how the family wouldn't have been happy with him no matter what name he used.

The next evening, after ranch chores, the two men occupied the chairs on the porch and chatted. Carl commented, "I've often wondered if you made it back to friendly lines and back to the States alive."

"I've had the same thoughts about you too. After we split up, there was no way of ever knowing." Carl reiterated his story of helping various fishermen while working his way south, working and living with Chi Lou Mei, and finally making it to Singapore. There he worked in a Chinese warehouse until he got a job on a freighter headed for Manila and San Francisco. Kyle explained, "South Vietnamese sympathizers smuggled me back to friendly lines.

After telling Kyle about Donna and his first ranch--which was now deeded to Mike and Sharon--and how the family turned out, Kyle started in with his life after returning from Vietnam. He had gotten married right after high school and had George, their son. Two years later he was drafted and joined the Navy. They put him in the Seabees, where he operated heavy equipment and repaired much of the same. He continued, "After I returned, life wasn't the same. Mary and I couldn't get along, nothing went right. The only friends I had were fellow veterans, and we tried to get together every Friday night at somebody's house.

Since I had a garage, most of the guys liked to come over to my place, kick a tire, tell stories, and drink beer. Mary couldn't stand my night owl ways or so many other things I did. She eventually got a divorce and took George with her. She moved to California, remarried, and passed away some years later."

Kyle continued, "According to Rachel, George--her father--married Cindy, and five years after Rachel was born, George was killed in an auto accident. Rachel was in seventh grade when she ran away from home and came to live with me. Something took place because she refused to go back. She's never told me why she detests her step dad. After she graduated from high school, she attended college and got summer jobs at Yellowstone, so I never saw her much after her graduation. To this day I don't know why she left her mother's, but I have an idea it might have had something to do with the guy her mother was living with.

In any case, being a truck driver created some real issues, so during the summers, I would send her to Seattle where she would live with my sister. They helped me raise her and I would have her during the school year because my truck routes were shorter. Once she graduated, she went on to college. She'd get jobs in other towns so I didn't see her anymore."

Carl interjected, "Sounds like you made it work and she turned out to be a very nice young lady."

Kyle brought Carl back to their days in Vietnam with the question, "Carl, do you ever think our Lord had something to do with our escape and our getting back home? Do you think it was our Lord who made sure we didn't get transferred from the forward camp to the Hanoi Hotel? Escape from there was almost impossible, you know."

"Bad things happened to us but look at the good things--we both escaped, we both returned home, we both have been able to make good with our lives. You ever think that didn't *just* happen?"

Carl replied, "I'm not sure, but yes, I do believe we have a friend someplace. Was it our Guardian Angel and he stopped for coffee the day the PRB was ambushed? Like you, I don't believe I'd have made it back on my own, much less made it back before my aunt passed away. You're right; too many things took place to have just happened by chance." After a moment of silence between the two, Carl glanced at Kyle and asked, "Where was my angel when I had to kill the soldier at the VC outpost?"

Kyle responded, "Maybe you were my angel."

Carl scoffed and added, "You mean the angels were off trying to save some hippie girl's virginity at the love-in and left me to my own devices. The angels shouldn't have allowed those men to be where they were when we encountered them. I didn't have a choice."

Kyle replied, "The Lord works in strange ways; he made sure we got home though he didn't make it easy."

"Easy! Hell, he's marked our souls so we can't sleep at night. Is it his way of reminding us every night of our past deeds? Hopefully it's our penance and not a preview of the hell coming to us later," was Carl's response.

Kyle replied, "The Lord forgives us, but we have to ask for that forgiveness."

While Carl and Kyle were chatting on the porch, Susan decided to take the coffee pot to them and refill their mugs.

Susan reached for the door knob to open the door, she heard Kyle commenting, "Stumbling into the Viet Cong soldier at the jungle outpost scared the shit out of me and you killed him with nothing but your hands before I had time to shit."

Susan froze, a cold shiver moved across her shoulders and down her spine. Goosebumps followed as they went down each arm. She didn't move as the thought hit her, *Carl's hands have at one time or another touched every inch of my body.*

She heard Carl reply, "I've relived that shit, a million times. I hate that dream; it's like having to see a bad movie over and over. I've spent many nights out on the porch drinking coffee so I wouldn't have to see that dream one more time."

Susan knew Carl spent many nights on the porch drinking coffee, and often wondered why. She also felt guilty eavesdropping like this, but she also walked into the conversation by accident.

Kyle added, "Mary never understood, and it ripped our marriage apart. I couldn't sleep--hell, I didn't want to sleep. Between my dreams and my drinking friends, there was never a happy moment in our house so she left me and took George with her."

Susan made some noises before opening the door and brought the coffee pot out and asked, "Are you two ready for a refill."

Both men replied, "Yes, by all means, thanks," as she refilled their coffee mugs.

Kyle changed the subject and continued, "You'll never know what went through my mind the moment your gravelly voice came over the CB. Your 'Dung Ho Pit.' sent chills all the way from my head to my butt. And to find both you and Rachel parked on the roadside, what a pleasant surprise."

Carl replied, "I didn't know of any other way to get the right person to stop. I figured if it wasn't you, the truck wouldn't stop, but if it was the Kyle I escaped with and that didn't get you to stop, nothing would."

Susan walked into the kitchen to make another pot of coffee. She thought that the two men might want to talk for a few more hours, and if not, oh well. She remembered the rough-and-tumble boy in her class who, as she remembered, wasn't popular but was never teased like she was. She also remembered hearing of a few of the fights he was in. She never doubted the rumors because she could still remember some of the boys having a black eye or noticeable bruises. Sometimes it was Carl who had the black eye, sometimes it was one of the other boys. She recalled, *As classmates, why didn't we ever talk to each other? We were both ostracized in some form from the standpoint of our classmates. None of them would befriend us.* It made her feel guilty because she also remembered Carl's rough-and-tumble attitude and it didn't appeal to her. As a teenager, she didn't know how to deal with that sort of person and didn't have the tools to help her see what Carl actually was. Well, until he broke Deric's arm and nose in her defense.

My God, what don't I know about him and his service in Vietnam? She remembered her discussion with her brother Howard back at the time Carl helped him rebuild the feed shed and what he said: "Carl survived more crap in Vietnam than most people see in a lifetime."

Her mind went to his recent helping with the ranch. He moved in like a roommate because it was more convenient than driving home every night and helped out. They slowly fell in love, and she didn't know what she would do without him now. *What hell was he reliving? All those times she found him sitting on the porch drinking coffee at all hours of the morning, always after midnight.*

Kyle continued, "I met Dan, a man who also served in country and helped me put things in perspective. If it hadn't been for his help, I'd have never been able to help Rachel during those years she lived with me. I wear this cross every day of my life to remind me of my Lord. After Mary left me, my life was in shambles; I quit drinking and gave my troubles to God. It was hard and I lost a lot of my friends, but as Dan said, things would get better. They did, Carl, they really did. Rachel came to live with me and I got better and better truck runs. I couldn't quite smoking. Sometimes the Lord asks too much of us, but he hasn't asked me to stop smoking."

Carl replied, "I'm happy life turned out well for you. Each veteran has his own way of coping, and some of them aren't good, and nothing more than smokescreens. I found the cabin I remember telling you about and moved into it. As Lady Luck would have it, I met Donna, my first wife. I loved her from the bottom of my heart. It's her daughter from a previous marriage and Mike, my nephew, who own and run the Weston Ranch now. That's where I was raised." With a big smile Carl commented, "I got to walk her down the aisle at their wedding."

Since Susan had gone to bed, Carl went in to check on the coffee. He returned and told Kyle, "If you wish, there's lots of coffee still on, so it you wish to stay up, feel free. I'm turning in, so I'll see you in the morning."

On Memorial Day, the town had a special program along with the local VFW. There were more people in attendance then Carl was comfortable with but he wanted to attend with Kyle. Several people who knew Carl found it interesting that he attended.

Susan held Carl's hand all through the program and could feel his distress and emotional moments at times. She purposely never let go of his hand. She wanted him to know she was with him, loved him, and wanted him. Susan was aware of the times Carl didn't hold her hand, the VFW called "parade rest," at which time Carl and Kyle would move to a different posture and the VFW announced "attention," both men stood at attention.

During "Taps," both men gave the solute, and during the prayer, both men removed their hats and bowed their heads.

When the prayer was done, Susan noticed Carl's hand

found hers without her trying to find his. She couldn't help herself and gave his hand a squeeze as hard as she could. By the time "Taps" was finished, Kyle had tears in his eyes, Susan mused, *It's too bad Rachel isn't here to hold his hand.*

38

TERRY

Carl was in town grocery shopping and decided to have a sandwich at the café. Deric finished his lunch and as he walked by Carl, he commented, "I see one of your buddies has posted the land everyone likes to ride their off-road rigs on."

This was news to Carl, the land to the east of the Weston's ranch and north of Susan's was open range and nobody used it due to it being poor ground. Most of it was used by quite a few motorcycle and ATV riders who liked to ride the many hills and ravines. If somebody bought it, it was the new owner's prerogative to allow others access.

While returning with the groceries, Carl stopped at the ranch to talk to Mike and see if he knew who the new neighbor was. After saying hello to both Sharon and Mike, he asked what the new of his new neighbor.

Mike's reply was, "As far as I know a veteran about your age and his father bought the land and moved a trailer house onto it. He also posted the land, so everybody's mad at them now. The other day while I was in town, I was told, 'The guy's a recluse, just like your father-in-law.' As I understand, they never go into town."

While eating dinner, Carl informed Susan they had a new neighbor to the north of them. Susan didn't mind because Carl made sure the fences were well maintained. She asked, "Should I take something up to them? Maybe something for the fellow's father since he'll be in his late eighties or early nineties?"

Carl suggested, "No, I'd leave them be; there's a reason they chose to live alone. *I know that feeling...*"

It was easy for Susan to accept Carl's suggestion since so many people hadn't given her their time of day while growing up. *Let the other person make the first move,* was her idea.

Carl was so busy with Susan's ranch he realized he'd forgotten to ride the Weston ranch fence line. The next day he got his gear prepared and left after breakfast. Riding along the east fence line in a northern direction, he checked for any repairs needing to be made. He finally came to a damaged section and while fixing it got the strange notion someone or something was watching him. While he worked, he watched what he was doing but let his eyes scan the area, looking for anything that might have given him the creepy feeling. After a few minutes, he detected a person two hundred yards away and on a hill overlooking his position. The person wasn't sky lined at the top of the hill but was halfway from the top. The person was also utilizing the foliage to mask his presents and movements. The hills to the east were more arid and brushier than the better pasture land located deeper in the valley floor.

Carl ignored him and finished repairing the fence, rode on to the next area where a fence post needed to be replaced. While working at this location, Carl noticed the person had obviously shadowed his movement and was now within a hundred yards but was still keeping hidden as best he could. Carl presumed it is was his new neighbor and wondered why he was so interested in what he was doing.

The person stepped into plain view at fifty yards. As he approached, he finally spoke, "Hi, are you the guy they told me about in town who owns the Weston Ranch?"

Carl replied, "Nope, my daughter and her husband own it." The other fellow was wearing camo clothes and a pair of binoculars hung from his neck.

The other man came closer and finally extended his

hand. "I'm Terry, and I'm glad to see you maintain the fence between us."

Carl grunted a gravelly "Carl," as he shook his neighbor's hand.

"I've heard of you in town."

Carl commented, "Believe what you wish, but most of what you hear probably isn't true."

Terry could understand that since most people misunderstood him also. He added, "I'm going to have to fence my north property line to keep people out. Too many people think they own it and access it any time they wish."

"Yup, I've heard some people are upset with you because of that."

"Doesn't some woman own the ranch south of me?"

"Yup, name's Susan Weston."

"I see where you have several locations where there are gates in this eastern boundary of yours. They don't appear to be gates, but in some respects, they are. You don't access this land, do you?" Terry asked

"No, but you're correct. I have several spots where if a person needs to cross this fence, there are locations they can. If someone gets in an emergency situation, it doesn't pay to not be able to get through the fence. A wildfire would be an excellent example." Terry didn't have a reply for that.

His neighbor watched him fix the fence and replace the fencepost before he spoke again. "You were in 'Nam too?"

"Yup, and a POW," replied Carl.

As Terry turned to leave, he replied, "Don't work too hard. I have to go check on my dad."

Terry hiked back to his house. He thought to himself, *so that's the Carl they told me about in town. I wasn't prepared for what I saw. He said he was a POW, and I know I'm lucky to have survived the war, but the treatment in those camps wasn't any cakewalk. I'll bet his face and voice are part of his prison treatment.*

Terry knew life wasn't going to be any better in Montana than it was in Colorado. He had married before he was drafted and their second little girl was born while he was in Vietnam. When he returned, his wife couldn't stand his being up all night, prowling the property at all hours of the day or night, or his crazy thrashing in bed when he did sleep. She discovered he trusted nobody and tended to embrace the life of a recluse. After three years of it, she left and took the girls. After that, Terry lived alone in the country until he lost everything in a house fire. Terry convinced his father to move to Montana where they could buy land and live off the grid.

So far, everything was working for them; although, while installing their new trailer house, a group of off road bikers rode right into their unimproved yard. The thought of those guys being able to get in on him while he was working on the house both frightened and infuriated him. How could he have missed those trails? Terry purposely located the home site a mile from the public road and behind the base of a hill so it couldn't be seen from the road.

The day he went out to the northern part of his property to stop some four-wheeler ATV riders, he knew he was opening a can of worms, but they had to understand it was his property now. At sixty-six years old, Terry was no spring chicken, but his father Stanley, who was in his late 80's, was not doing so well. Terry had to straighten the house after him and keep an eye on him. Stanley bankrolled the house and land, and Terry helped him get along with his day-to-day life. Stanley was quite shaky now, but he loved the outdoors.

It took Terry three months to finish fencing his north and east boundary. Luckily he was able to tie into the Weston's north boundary fence and the north end of Susan's east boundary fence. While working at the end of his property, he took time to quietly explore part of Susan's property. Terry wanted to know who his neighbors were, but he darn well wasn't going to visit their home and make introductions.

Right after some autumn rains, Deric, Roger, Steve,

and Pete went riding their motorbikes and cut the fence so they could ride the hills they always loved to ride.

After an hour of riding, Terry was waiting for them at the location where they had cut the fence. He threatened them with a rifle and informed them to never come back. Deric was livid and confronted Terry. Terry wasn't going to take any crap from the trespassers, so he mashed the butt of his rifle into Deric's ribs. This knocked Deric off his bike and knocked the wind out of him.

As Deric hit the ground, Terry turned and faced the other three in case they wanted to join the party. Once Deric remounted his bike, the three rode through the break in the fence.

Terry fixed the fence the next day. It was pouring rain, and it didn't help his foul mood.

A WEEK LATER, while Carl and Susan were having dinner with Mike and Sharon, Mike informed Carl of the confrontation between the bike riders and their new neighbor.

Carl commented, "His name's Terry. I met him a while back. I was riding the fence line and he said he was living with his father. I drove by there the other day and it looks like they've put a trailer house behind one of those hills so it's not visible from the road. Much like our northern section, they have a gate so people can't access their place either."

Mike added, "All I know is rumor has it the guy's crazy."

Carl replied, "Yup, crazy, just like all the rest of the Vietnam veterans aren't. It's the same old story. A guy wants to be left alone, and suddenly he's crazy."

Both Mike and Sharon knew exactly how frustrating this was for Carl. Mike's return from Afghanistan was nothing like that of the Vietnam veterans.

Susan didn't often take the county road off to the east of her ranch, but she was driving to another ranch to get some produce, much like she used to do when Donna, Carl's first wife, used to have her produce stand. She was five miles from anything and encountered an elderly man walking the road. Being this far from the nearest driveway, she stopped and asked if he was okay.

He appeared to not know or remember where he was. He asked, "Are you Betty?"

Susan replied, "No, but can I take you home?" Susan made a quick guess; *I wonder if this is the new neighbor or his father*? They lived some miles back, so she offered him a ride. She drove him back and parked at the gate. While she was walking with him along the driveway to the house, they met Terry. He was obviously distressed, discovering his father was being brought home by some woman he didn't know.

Susan explained she found his father two miles up the road and he didn't know here he was.

Terry was relieved to see his father and desperately wondered, *how can I keep Dad from walking off again*? Terry thanked Susan and also noticed she wasn't any beauty queen. *I know a pretty woman when I see one, and this gal sure doesn't qualify.*

Susan asked, "When I stopped to talk to him, he asked me if I was Betty?"

"Betty's my ex-wife's name. He might have thought you were she. Dad lived with the two of us for several years." Terry didn't want this woman hanging around so added, "Thank you for bringing him back, I'm sorry you had to take time out of your day." With that, he reached for his father's arm and steered him towards the house with their backs to the woman and her car.

Terry solved the problem of his father by installing a small fence around the house. The latch was sophisticated and hard to operate so Stanley couldn't get out.

The biggest issue was the latching mechanism was hard to operate in the dark, and Terry didn't always stay in the house much less in the yard after dark. When he remembered the Huey helicopters dropping his platoon in enemy territory--or the time they were ambushed by the

North Vietnamese Army and they had to fight their way back to a helicopter retrieving area in his mind--he was beside himself. He had to get out of the house, he had to get away, and he had to find some place quiet to be alone. The dreams came less frequently now, but they still visited him at night, the time their evacuation Huey got hit by enemy fire and went down was one of the worst.

People seldom survived from a downed bird, but somehow he'd been thrown clear. He thought he was a goner as the enemy closed in and continued to shoot at the crashed Huey. When the enemy fire continued to hit it, the fuel tanks went up and nothing was left. The squad of men detailed to get any survivors, got to him as the bird exploded. That dream always comes back and there's no escaping, he's lying in the brush with bullets flying everywhere. The NVA was getting close and they would kill him, the bird exploded. The noise, the crash, and the gut-churning fear always returned. Yes, the solitude and quiet of the night was his only help, that and a few bottles of beer.

39

LISA AND LAURA

Terry was fixing dinner for him and his father when he heard a vehicle approach. The gate was locked, so somebody had to have cut the chain or the lock to gain entry. To say the least, he was instantly angered. Looking out the window, he saw the sheriff fumbling with the yard gate latch. Terry grabbed his jacket and went outside to ask why the officer was on his property. The sheriff was still fumbling with the latch as Terry reached the gate and demanded, "What brings you here?"

The sheriff replied, "I need to take a look around."

Terry responded, "You're not welcome, so if you feel you have cause to search my property, you need a search warrant."

The sheriff replied, "I see you have quite the child-proof latch on this gate."

Terry learned years ago never to give more information than necessary, so he didn't say anything, nor did he mention the gate was to keep his aging and forgetful father from walking away or on the highway again.

The sheriff looked at Terry and said, "Your non-cooperation won't go well for you. A second grade school girl was abducted earlier today and you live the closest to where she gets off her school bus."

Terry replied, "I don't know what you're accusing me of, but if you cut the lock on my gate, I expect you to replace it."

The sheriff left, Terry figured he'd have approximately an hour to an hour and a half to do some searching on his own to see if the girl was on his land. Why or what she could be doing there was beyond him, but he'd at least look. He went back inside, donned his camo, and hiked several of the hills between his house and driveway, towards where the other ranch driveway was located on the opposite side of the highway. Terry's three strand fence wasn't people-proof; if somebody wanted to get through it, they could as it was a deterrent. Any child or small girl could easily fit between the fence strands. The biggest issue was why would a child do that?

Or did somebody grab her and bring her onto my land? Granted, he'd made some enemies, but who would do this?

Terry returned to his house twenty minutes before the sheriff who was accompanied by two other cars containing three officers and a woman, whom Terry presumed to be a social worker. The sheriff produced the search warrant and demanded entry. Terry gestured with his hand they could enter, but he didn't help them with the gate latch. After some fumbling, one of the other officers managed to get it open. As the day ended, it became too dark to search the surrounding land, but the officers scoured his house and shop.

By this time the officers had been notified that two girls were missing. The officers didn't find any sign of the girls, and as they prepared to leave, the sheriff told Terry, "You're in more trouble than you think, and when we find where you've hidden the girls, this isn't going to go well for you. I'm going to get your neighbor, Carl Weston, and his horses to help us comb every inch of your land. We'll be back."

Terry picked up on the "girls," N*ow there's two missing?* In his mind, he wanted to crawl into a hole. *How could this be happening to him; what did he ever do to deserve this?* He instantly felt the urge to puke and didn't know what to do or where to turn; he didn't have a friend he could talk to.

As he walked back into the house, he slammed his fist against the door and slammed it behind him.

On the way back to town, the sheriff stopped at Susan's ranch and asked Carl if they could use his horses for a search.

Carl informed them it would have to be in daylight hours because his horses weren't trained for night riding, and besides, it would take some time to get them ready for an extended outing. He was more than happy to help search for the two girls and asked. "Are you sure they are on Terry's land?"

"Once they got off the bus, the closest place to take and hide them is his land. They could have been taken after the bus drove off but before they had time to walk home."

"How sure are you it was Terry? I take it nobody saw an abduction take place, so you don't know if somebody picked them up with a car and they're a hundred miles from here by now."

The sheriff replied, "You're right, we have no witnesses.' I don't believe what you voiced took place. Terry on the other hand..."

Before he had time to finish his statement, Carl added,

"Is half-crazy, I know. All of us Vietnam veterans are half crazy."

"Dammit Carl, we've had this conversation before. That's not what I'm saying," replied the sheriff.

"The hell it isn't. I've been on the receiving end of your shit myself, if you will recall. If you don't wish to remember, allow me to refresh your memory. It was over a trespasser's motorcycle. If you're not happy with that incident, remember the barn fire we had."

"Dammit Carl, will you let us use your horses?" demanded the sheriff.

"Yes, but I'm the hostler and you guys ride. Good luck finding the girls, Sheriff," Carl meant this last and didn't mind helping.

While eating dinner, Carl explained the situation to Susan.

Susan replied, "Terry has his father living with him. What would he ever do with two small children?" Carl agreed with her and replied, "I'm sure glad Terry has his dad living with him. Loneliness can be a bitter companion."

The next morning at day break, three officers met Carl with his horses and headed out to Terry's land. Carl took them to one of the not-so-obvious gates and accessed Terry's land. The officers still had their search warrants, and Carl took them into a military-style search pattern.

By halfway through the day, the officers hated themselves and Carl. None of them had ever ridden horses before, so it was a grueling day. They wished they could stop, but Carl wasn't going to spend a second day with them, and besides, *"If they're on Terry's land we'll find them today."*

Carl took them north along the fence line and doubled back so they could search more territory in the fastest and easiest way. While in the northern portion of Terry's land, they could see all the bike and quad paths, including where they used to cross onto Terry's land. Carl didn't say a word, but wanted the officers to realize where so much animosity came from concerning certain individuals in town.

Continuing the search for the girls, the group was slowly working their way into a small ravine where Carl planned on letting the horses drink from a small stream. As they rounded a bend, two girls came into sight, screaming in delight.

"That bastard, Terry lied about the kids. And he's left them out here." proclaimed the sheriff.

The two little girls ran up to the horses and Carl dismounted before they could get too close because he didn't want them too close to the horse's legs and have them get hurt. Carl let everybody dismount while the horses drank, and they finally got the story out of the girls.

They were frightened, lost, and happy to be found. They ran away so they wouldn't have to go back to school the next day and they could spend the day playing. When they got off the school bus, rather than going to Laura's house, the two girls crossed the county road, climbed through the fence, and hiked over several hills so nobody would see them. After they lost sight of the road and all the hills looked the same to them, they didn't know which way to go back. They found the little creek so they had water, but they were hungry and scared.

They also started bawling because they were going to be in trouble for running away. They weren't sure if they should go home. The officers explained both their mothers and fathers were worried and wanted them home as soon as possible.

Carl put the two girl's fear to rest with the idea of getting to ride his horse. Once he got both girls on his horse, he patted the horse's neck and told the girls, "This is Sheila. She likes giving people rides, so she's going to like giving the two of you a ride." Carl had to smile at himself; *the horse would prefer the two little girls any day to his fat butt*. He walked while leading the group to Terry's house where he could use Terry's driveway to take the horses to the county road, and from there, over to the

Morton's ranch where Laura lived. Lisa's parents could meet them there to get their daughter.

Once more Terry had the urge to puke at the sight of Carl leading the group of three officers on horseback and the two girls. This isn't going to go well. *How did those kids get on my land? Who would do this to me? I see they conscripted the neighbor guy with his horses to help too. If this turns as ugly as I think it will, what will I do about Dad?*

There was a second reason Carl took this path; he wanted Terry to be the first to know he wasn't culpable. He also darn well wanted the sheriff to have to make face-to-face amends with Terry. Carl didn't know the whole story, but from comments the sheriff made, he could tell the sheriff thought Terry was somehow involved in the girls' disappearance.

Carl asked Terry if he wanted to go with them while taking the girls home. "No, but the sheriff needs to replace the lock he cut. He could have walked to the house, he can walk. Terry's reply didn't surprise Carl.

The Morton's were excited and happy with the return of their daughter and phoned the Helmsley's, Lisa's parents, so they could come over and get their daughter. They all thanked Carl for helping find the girls while Lisa and Laura petted Sheila.

By the end of the day, the officers could hardly walk

and couldn't wait to get home to shower and clean up. Each one hated the smell of horses by this time.

Carl took time to explain to each girl's parents to watch for any health issues that might crop up. He explained, since they drank the water from the stream, they could get Beaver fever, or giardia, so if they get diarrhea that wouldn't stop, get them to a doctor because it won't go away in a few days. It takes antibiotics to kill it.

Debbie, Lisa's mother, realized it wasn't the officers who found the girls; it was Carl with his horses. The rumors she heard through the years weren't exactly what one would consider honorable, yet here he was, helping search for other people's children. W*hy did they choose him, he wasn't the only rancher who had horses*. Carl wasn't a young man either. He was old enough to be her father.

Carl still had to get the horses home, unsaddled, fed, watered, and brushed. They worked hard and deserved their dinner, getting cleaned, brushed, and a cozy night in their stalls. Carl couldn't wait for his dinner either, but the horses came first. It was well after dark when he walked into the house and Susan put his dinner on the table for him. "Water will have to do because I'm not going to make coffee." She said as, she gave him a hug and added, "I'm so happy you found the girls."

Carl agreed, "I'm glad there won't be a news article

about some crazy veteran abducting two little girls. That's all we don't need. A hot shower is going to feel so good."

Once asleep for the night, Carl dreamt the time he and Chi Lou Mei were low on money and the engine was in need of new parts. Carl was surprised when they took on board a man with three young girls. They left port and took the four from Thailand to the next port south, which was in Malaysia. When they moored beside the ship and the four were to get off, the man got in an argument with Chi Lou Mei over payment or the fact he also wanted to buy her young girl. The moment Chi Lou Mei pulled her long Kris dagger from where he didn't know, but he also quickly grabbed a fair-sized crescent wrench, and with both armed boatmen, the man got quiet and didn't push the issue.

The ship was registered in Oman and his stomach wanted to empty itself. He could feel the bile entering his throat as he contemplated where the girls were probably being taken. Damn, he hated his part in this but if he wanted to see home again, he had to shut up and carry on. Chi Lou Mei needed money for her boat badly, but man; she was sure taking a chance. Crossing international borders with human cargo—and it was most likely sex slave trafficking--would land them in jail forever.

The minute the man and girls boarded the other vessel, Chi Lou Mei cast off and set sail. Carl never spoke, always staying with the engine or doing the manual labor on her boat. He would protect her with his life because she was his only hope of ever reaching a port where he could get passage back to the States. Having a knife fight on her boat wouldn't be pretty, so his goal would have been to smash the man's head before he hurt Chi Lou Mei.

In his dream, at the moment Chi Lou Mei pulled the knife and he grabbed the wrench, he woke, bathed in sweat as if he were once more in the tropics, and in the act of ripping the covers off trying to get at the man to smash his head before he could hurt Chi Lou Mei.

He wouldn't sleep any more -- so he headed for the kitchen to fix coffee. He'd sit on the porch and try to cool and calm his overreacting body and mind.

THE FOLLOWING SUNDAY, the Helmsleys stopped at Carl and Susan's so they could have Lisa personally thank Carl. Carl also took her to the barn and let her see the horses again and she could pet Sheila.

While Carl and Lisa were in the barn, Lisa's grandmother, Becky commented to Susan, "It's been so many years since we've seen each other. Where does the time go?"

Susan replied, "It's so nice of you to stop by and thank Carl."

Becky added, "Carl would have made a wonderful father."

Susan didn't know how to take this comment since as far as Carl and Sharon were concerned, they were remarkably close. She was his daughter though he wasn't her biological father—he had adopted her after all. Or was Becky commenting on the fact Susan had never had any children? It was a topic Susan didn't like to talk about because she would have loved to have had a child or two, but it never took place.

Becky sensed Susan's cool reception and wondered why she was so aloof; it sure made it hard to break the ice with her. Becky recalled the dowdy long dresses Susan always wore to school and she never joined the girls after school.

Susan's guarded answers didn't escape Becky and to her, Susan was being hard to get to know. Obviously, she hadn't changed at all since they were in school. Susan recognized Lisa's Grandmother Becky as one of her classmates who never gave her the time of day, never included her, and did her share of teasing. Susan tried to forgive, but it was hard and it didn't mean you had to be welcoming either. It was Becky's place to make the first move.

Lisa was jumping up and down with excitement after getting to see the horses again; especially getting to feed Sheila some oats and pet her.

Carl started a conversation with Richard, Lisa's father, and the two of them talked ranching for a half hour while the ladies struggled.

Debbie, Lisa's mother also told Carl and Susan of the discussion they had with Lisa about making good decisions and not always going along with friends or others who suggest doing things, especially when you know it's going to get you in trouble.

Lisa was uncomfortable with this because she knew her mother still tucked her in at night, read her a story, and said prayers with her before she went to bed, but she also had extra chores to do, chores she didn't have to do before. She also questioned how good of a friend Laura was after she hatched the idea of running away so they could play all day instead of attending school. Lisa new she had allowed her friend to lead her into the idea of skipping school and she knew she'd remember it for the rest of her life, especially how scared she was when they discovered they were lost, didn't have any food to eat, and spent the night in the cold hugging each other trying to keep warm.

After returning home, Becky paged through one of her lower class annuals and found Carl's picture. After looking at the photo for a couple of moments, she remembered him as she had known him back in school. As she recalled, he didn't have many friends and was often in trouble. Oh yes, now she remembered, Deric Hollingsworth was teasing Susan and for no reason, Carl broke Deric's arm and smashed his face. Well, he got what he deserved, expelled from school. So he ended up in Vietnam like so many others who couldn't qualify to get into college. What baffled her was why he helped the sheriff hunt for the girls.

A week later Terry stopped by and Susan opened the door.

"Is Carl available," he asked.

Susan replied, "He might be in the barn."

A half hour later Carl and Terry returned and on entering the house, Carl motioned towards the table and said, "Have a seat," as he put coffee on.

They talked and had three cups of coffee when Terry stood up to leave, "I have to get back and check on my dad."

As he was leaving, Carl remarked, "Don't make yourself a stranger, you're welcome any time."

Terry turned and replied, "I'm honored to know you as a brother in arms. You look after your people; I have to look after mine."

40

RACHEL'S WEDDING

Rachel was on her way back to Minnesota from Seattle for a summer job when she stopped in to see Susan and Carl. After dinner and catching up, Susan and Carl had her stay the night. After breakfast she was on the road again.

SIX MONTHS LATER, she phoned Susan and asked if she could plan a wedding to be held on their ranch. Susan got excited and asked when she would get to meet the lucky guy. Rachel took care of most of the planning but kept Susan informed so there wouldn't be any conflicts with the schedule or where out-of-town guests would stay.

Rachel would stay at their house in the spare room

and use the main bedroom as her bridal room. Rachel's grandfather, Kyle, would stay at Mike and Sharon's ranch.

The day of the May wedding was sunny and warm. While getting everything ready, Susan prepared many of the dishes for the reception to be held right after the wedding. This wasn't a big chore since there wouldn't be many people attending. Shortly before the ceremony, Susan went to her room, joined Rachel and her maid of honor, and changed clothes.

Susan returned downstairs, Carl saw her new dress and a completely different hairstyle than she'd ever worn before, and remarked, "Wow, you're stunning. Are you going to outshine the bride?"

Susan beamed at Carl's reaction and new it was genuine from his tone of voice. At Carl's comment, her tummy took a flip flop, so happy because for once, somebody thought she was pretty. Carl was taken by her looks. Her large silver Navajo earrings with their touch of red coral and bluish turquoise complemented her red dress. Her black hair framing her earrings made them shine, removing all regard from her plain facial features.

Carl's first thought was, *Whose big day is this going to be?* Obviously, Susan's glowing smile was testament to how much she was going to enjoy this day. *Wow,* Carl reflected. *She doesn't smile like that very often.*

Two of Rachel's college friends provided music for the ceremony with a keyboard and flute accompaniment.

Kyle--wearing a black suit, white shirt, black tie, still wearing his large silver cross hanging on his chest--walked his granddaughter down the aisle. Her maid of honor was a classmate and a good friend. The groom's brother was the best man.

Since parents get to sit in the front row, Rachel had her grandpa sit next to the aisle with his sister, her aunt from Seattle, seated next to him. Rachel also put Susan and Carl in the front row, they had become family. They did more for her at a moment in her life when she needed help, and she would never be able to repay what it meant to her. She could stop in any time she wished and they treated her like a daughter.

Seated next to Carl was her mother, Cindy, who from her expression wasn't happy about the seating arrangement. It didn't escape Carl by her facial expressions she displayed the moment he remarked to her, "Good afternoon," as he took his seat beside her since she had been seated first.

The groom's father provided a case of beer and wine for the reception. Susan made sure there was plenty of punch, tea, and coffee available too. Sharon joined Susan and Rachel's girlfriends for some friendly getting to know each other and reconnecting with each other.

Kyle gravitated to Carl, and while they chatting, Mike joined them. Mark, the groom's father, joined them and made sure each one had a beer. Carl had previously made sure Kyle had coffee. Carl accepted the one beer but reverted back to coffee as soon as he finished the beer. The ladies definitely enjoyed the wine. Mark had never been on a ranch before and was surprised at how nice such a small wedding in a farmyard could be.

Carl used Susan's expression and said, "You've been living in the city too long."

The four men were chatting for a few minutes and several comments got made referring to the service.

Kyle remarked, "Every person who served is marked: there's always a mark on the inside but sometimes there's one on the outside too."

Mark wasn't sure how to react because he considered the remark, uncalled for. He interpreted it as verbal pointing to Carl's scarred face and terrible voice. He didn't know it, but Carl was comfortable with Kyle's remark because in many ways, he was correct. It was something you expect from a close veteran friend. In reality, the remark was aimed at each one of them.

Mark wanted to change the topic, so while facing Kyle he said, "I thought you were the preacher and not the parent."

"Grandfather in this case." replied Kyle. "Me, a

chaplain? Oh you're hilarious. You're courting a lightning strike talking like that," remarked Kyle while laughing and spilling some of his coffee.

The use of the word "chaplain" triggered an internal reminder in Mark's brain and he added, "I take it you also served?"

Kyle replied while indicating Carl, "We met in Vietnam."

Carl indicated Mike and added, "Afghanistan."

This revelation put Mark at ease for now he understood these men. He replied, "I was on the *Kitty Hawk* deck crew for the A4's."

Kyle remarked, "Two snipes and an Airedale: what a group we make. Sorry, Mike, you were in the Army."

Snipes are Navy engineering personnel who work below decks—enginemen, boiler men, and repairmen. Airedales are Navy personnel who work with aircraft, especially those who work on aircraft carriers such as the *USS Kitty Hawk*.

Susan approached and accosted the four men. "I see you're trying to hide from the other guests, I'm not going to allow you to stand around the beer cooler all by yourselves." She wanted them to mingle though she knew it would be hard for Carl. One thing she appreciated, both Carl and Kyle were drinking coffee while Mark and Mike were both having a beer.

Later after the party while holding both of Susan's hands, Carl commented, "I'm not sure which I prefer, you wearing your red dress and silver earrings or your pajamas."

Susan replied with a smile, "We can always test the pajama theory in the morning." *He's such a flirt and tease, but he always makes me happy,* she thought.

41

THE FOLLOWING SUMMER

After dinner Carl and Susan sat in their favorite seats on the front porch drinking coffee, Carl put his hand on Susan's hand. Susan presumed he wanting to say something.

After a few minutes, he opened with, "It was hard coming back to the States with no identity. All of our Vietnam veterans found it hard to return to such an ungrateful nation. The public's attitude didn't change until September 2011. Our veterans were never treated like that in the past and I hope it never happens again. Granted there was plenty of anti-war sentiment, but they shouldn't have taken it out on our men. Some of them went through hell and others didn't get to return. The stigma attached to us as a group as being half-crazy was heralded in the newspapers every chance they got. I know your brother dealt with it. Terry's still dealing with it; you could tell it in the way the sheriff treated him. Kyle is still living with it. Hell, PTSD destroyed his marriage. I know what it's like to want to crawl into a hole and be left alone. Donna was the best thing that happened to me. Damn, I hated losing her."

Susan squeezed his hand but didn't comment.

Carl continued, "I'm so lucky; that shit didn't hit me as bad as most guys.

Susan replied, "Are you sure about that? Why do I still find you sitting out here on the porch at two, three, or four in the morning drinking coffee?"

Carl didn't answer because he knew she was too close for comfort, she was right.

Susan didn't want to open any sore wounds but had to ask, "Why did you stop Deric the way you did when he took my purse?"

Carl was quiet for a few minute before he replied, "Daric's a jerk. We had our altercations, and I couldn't stand him playing with you. The whole class was egging him on. It was as if you were a rat in the bucket to be played with. I didn't like him treating somebody who didn't have a chance and I guess I saw red. So as he ran past my desk, I snagged his arm, it was as if he hit a brick wall, and as his body twisted, his arm broke. I didn't know it because I was concentrating on was smashing his face. My fist hit his nose, and to this day he has a crooked nose. I knew it didn't matter what I did; I was going to be in trouble. So I nonchalantly walked to the front of the class and started helping you gather your stuff. My uncle shipped me off to a military style academy two weeks later. By the time I graduated, I knew I wasn't going to come back, so I joined the Navy."

Susan commented, "We weren't friends. You never talked to me; I didn't know what to think. Deric and so many others teased me all the time, but I've never been so humiliated in my life—never, that was the worst day of my life."

"My worst days were in the prison camp," Carl added.

Susan squeezed his hand, knowing he lost his voice while being tortured there. Hoping he wouldn't clam up, she asked. "Carl, how many men did you kill over there?"

He replied, "Being in the Navy, I was on board a destroyer most of the time, but when I was transferred to the PBR, I was the engineman and ran the engines. What the gunners' mates did with the machineguns; I have no idea. When ambushed, we shot back and called in helicopter support. What those gunships left behind; we never went back to find out."

Her next question frightened her, but she felt she needed to know. "I heard you talking to Kyle and he mentioned something about killing a guard?"

Carl was quiet for several minutes, and Susan thought he wasn't going to answer. Finally he answered, "Susan, when you're escaping from a prison camp, shit happens. It's either you or them.

After a long silence, Susan knew she wouldn't get any more information from him, so she changed the topic. "Carl, do you remember pulling my hair in second grade?"

Again Carl didn't answer right away but finally and sheepishly said, "Yes, I've never forgotten. I was sorry afterwards but it taught me an important lesson; never treat people bad if they don't deserve it. I've always hoped you wouldn't remember it."

Susan replied, "It sometimes takes a long time to forgive people after they treated you like a leper all through school. Dale was to me like Donna was to you. I don't know if it was fate or did our guardian angels bring us together, but I'm glad it happened."

Carl interjected, "Yeah, how about that? The two class misfits finally got together--who would have ever guessed? I'm still amazed at how you slowly sneaked into my heart."

Susan squeezed Carl's hand thinking, *Who sneaked into whose heart?*

How lucky I was to have the two nicest women stumble into my life, or did I stubble into theirs? contemplated Carl

With that thought, Carl smiled and squeezed Susan's hand again. Carl replied, "Life has had its obstacles, but I honestly feel, I'm home at last."

AUTHOR'S NOTE

Dear reader,

I tried to make my veterans suffering from Post-Traumatic Stress Disorder (PTSD) as real as I could. Not all returning veterans suffered from it, but for those who did and do, it's a genuine situation that affects them for the rest of their life. The media never focused on the fact most of our Vietnam veterans returned and became productive and successful citizens.

Some symptoms of PTSD are:

•Emotional detachment

•Anxiety and irritability

•Sleep or concentration difficulties

•Flashbacks and nightmares

•Lack of interest in social interaction and the avoidance of social engagements

•Angry, impulsive, or paranoid behavior

The struggle to sleep, flashbacks, and emotional detachment is portrayed in my characters Carl and Terry. Anxiety, irritability or anger and the struggle to sleep--including hostility and impulsive behavior--is portrayed in Terry. Terry and Carl both wanted to live an isolated life, exhibiting emotional detachment and a lack of socializing. Kyle experienced flashbacks, nightmares, and anxiety and irritability, which cost him his marriage. Howard, on the other hand, served in the USN Seabees and was able to return and become a unionized heavy equipment operator. Carl isolated himself on the ranch and avoided the corporate rat race but still became a productive rancher. Kyle lost his marriage before he found religion, pulled his life together, and became a successful big-rig truck driver. Terry, in his advanced age was still having problems with all of the symptoms listed above.

I hope you, my reader, enjoyed the book and have a new understanding of how so many of our returning Vietnam veterans were treated upon their return, and the erroneous stereotype the American public and media painted them with. Granted, the anti-war sentiment was at its highest, but that shouldn't have been a reason to treat our returning veterans--who did their duty and their nation's dirty work--so poorly and unjustly.

ABOUT THE AUTHOR

John Rhodes grew up in Wrangell, Alaska and joined the Navy in 1967. After two cruises on destroyers to the Tonkin Gulf of Vietnam, he was honorably discharged in 1970. In 1979, he earned his Bachelor of Science in Civil Engineering at the University of Idaho.

John retired in 2013 after working thirty-four years for the Washington State Department of Transportation. During that time John wrote many articles for sport magazines. After retiring, he started writing novels, always including veterans as the main characters.

ALSO BY JOHN H. RHODES

The Trespasser, the Rescue, and the Family

Made in the USA
Middletown, DE
19 May 2022

65931976R00195